THE GARDENS OF TANTALUS

AND OTHER DELUSIONS

I0676964

by

Brian Stableford

The Borgo Press
An Imprint of Wildside Press

MMVIII

CONTENTS

About the Author 4
Introduction 5

The Gardens of Tantalus 7
The Lost Romance 31
Lucifer's Comet 45
The Miracle of Zunderburg...................................54
The Cult of Selene..67
Ice and Fire...72
Self-Sacrifice..78
To the Bad..93
Riding the Tiger 104
Curiouser and Curiouser: A Kitchen Sink Drama
    by "Carol Lewis" 139
Quality Control 148
Worse Than the Disease.....................................188

ABOUT THE AUTHOR

BRIAN STABLEFORD was born in Yorkshire in 1948. He taught at the University of Reading for several years, but is now a full-time writer. He has written many science fiction and fantasy novels, including: *The Empire of Fear*, *The Werewolves of London*, *Year Zero*, *The Curse of the Coral Bride*, and *The Stones of Camelot*. Collections of his short stories include: *Sexual Chemistry: Sardonic Tales of the Genetic Revolution*, *Designer Genes: Tales of the Biotech Revolution*, and *Sheena and Other Gothic Tales*. He has written numerous nonfiction books, including *Scientific Romance in Britain, 1890-1950*, *Glorious Perversity: The Decline and Fall of Literary Decadence*, and *Science Fact and Science Fiction: An Encyclopedia*. He has contributed hundreds of biographical and critical entries to reference books, including both editions of *The Encyclopedia of Science Fiction* and several editions of the library guide, *Anatomy of Wonder*. He has also translated numerous novels from the French language, including several by the feuilletonist Paul Féval.

INTRODUCTION

Delusion is an enduring conviction that the world is other than it really is. It is arguable that conscious life would be unendurable were it not for the human capacity for delusion, and that existential *angst* would destroy us if we were not able to mount various kinds of pretended defense against the knowledge that our lives are utterly futile and bound to end in ignominious and painful death. Just as there are two kinds of people in the world—people who think that there are only two kinds of people in the world and people who don't—so there are two kinds of fiction: fiction that collaborates in the business of delusion and fiction that pretends not to. I write "pretends not to" rather than "doesn't" because, of course, the idea that fiction can somehow opt out of the business of delusion is itself a delusion. At the end of the day, there is no defense but pretence—although, by virtue of that very fact, it is not only useful but virtuous to pretend otherwise.

Most of the stories contained herein deal, directly or indirectly, with manifest delusions. By representing the delusions they feature *as* delusions, they promote the delusion that delusion can eventually be undermined by the strong-minded, who will thus be enabled to avoid the "bad faith" of which some existentialist philosophers seem to have lived in mortal terror. The ostensible purpose of this introduction is to remind readers to treat that implication with due skepticism—but the pretence that one can penetrate the pretence that pretence is penetrable, thus to reach a clearer conceptualization of the snares of delusion, is merely to advance into an infinite regress of self-delusion, and is probably best avoided. Sensible readers are, therefore, advised to skip this introduction altogether and take what meager comfort they can from the stories' earnest but ironic conviction that it is possible, even in a world as cruel as ours, to become a little wiser and a little more honest than the mediocre human average, merely by thinking cynically. If only....

Four of the stories included here first appeared in *Interzone*, "Self-Sacrifice" in issue number 53 (November 1991), "Riding the Tiger" in number 68 (February 1993), "Lucifer's Comet" in number 111 (September 1996) and "Worse Than the Disease" in number 113 (November 1996). "Riding the Tiger" had been written as a sequel to "To the Bad", which first appeared in *The Weerde: Book 1* (Roc, 1992), edited by Mary Gentle & Roz Kaveney, but it failed to make it into the second Weerde anthology (thus saving me the bother of lamenting the fact that no third one ever appeared). "The Gardens of Tantalus" first appeared in *Classical Whodunnits* (Past Times, 1996), edited by Michael Ashley. "The Lost Romance" first appeared in *The Chronicles of the Holy Grail* (Raven, 1996), also edited by Michael Ashley.

"The Cult of Selene" and "Ice and Fire" both appeared in *Albedo One*, the former in issue number 14 (1997) and the latter in number 18 (1999). "Curiouser and Curiouser: A Kitchen Sink Drama by Carol Lewis" and "The Miracle of Zunderburg" both appeared in *Redsine* 4 (February 2001). "Quality Control" first appeared in *The Mammoth Book of Dracula* (Robinson, 1997), edited by Stephen Jones.

—Brian Stableford
Reading, England

THE GARDENS OF TANTALUS

We live, it seems, in an Age of Miracles—or *lived* in one, at any rate, for the miracles about which the young men always seem to be talking all took place in their grandfathers' time, when Claudius, Nero, or Vespasian was emperor in Rome. Strange to relate, I—who am certainly a grandfather, born in the seventh year of Nero's rule—heard little or no talk of miracles at the time, when the word on all men's lips, in Corinth at least, was *philosophy.*

One rarely hears that word nowadays; it seems that men have a greater appetite for miracles.

My ignorance of the Age of Miracles through which I lived seems all the more remarkable when I recall—as clearly as if it were yesterday, although fifty years and more have passed—that I was present when one of the most widely-rumored miracles took place, and am named in all accounts as the benefactor of that miracle.

Lest any Christian should read this—although that seems unlikely, given that a literate Christian is almost a contradiction in terms—let me hasten to say that it is not one of the miracles of their beloved Jesus to which I refer. His crucifixion must have taken place near thirty years before I was born. The miracle-worker I was privileged to meet was a very different man: Apollonius of Tyana, whose associate Damis of Nineveh produced the memoir of his life that proclaimed him a great magician. What Damis sought to prove by this I do not know, but I do know that Apollonius would have despised him for it, for Apollonius was a true philosopher, who had no truck with magic, omens or gods.

So far as I can tell, the principal effect of Damis' fantasies has been to call forth hymns of hate from the followers

7

of Jesus, whose instinct is to damn all miracle-workers save their own as black magicians and addicts of the sinister. Apollonius has already been attacked in this wise by one Moeragenes, who never knew him at all. But I am only a white-beard philosopher, in a world where age and wisdom count for nothing. For all I know, the lies that Damis tells might secure the memory of Apollonius until the end of time, so that in a thousand years men will know nothing of his life except that he once wrought miracles, and saved a fool named Menippus from the wiles of a lamia.

Perhaps he did; perhaps it is I, Menippus, who am deluded into thinking the world a humdrum place, which might be understood if only men would put aside their silly obsessions with the naming of imaginary gods and the everpresent threat of demons.

* * * * * * *

I will admit that there is much in the memoir of Damis with which I can pick no quarrel. It may be revealing, however, that most of what seems to me to be true relates to matters of which neither Damis nor I had any direct knowledge, merely repeating the account that Apollonius gave of his own history.

Apollonius was born during the long reign of Augustus, at Tyana in Cappadocia. He was well-schooled and showed great precocity in the art of rhetoric. He became a philosopher of the school of Pythagoras and soon became notorious for preaching, according to the creed of that school, that animal sacrifice is a useless evil. He refused to eat meat, never wore any sandals save those made of bark, and wore no clothing save for that made of linen. He renounced his patrimony, refused all use of money, and once took a five-year vow of silence while he traveled the world.

This vow of silence added greatly to his reputation for holiness, which was responsible in its turn for the fact that so many people sought him out as a healer—but he told me that the reason for the vow was to make of himself a distanced observer, that he might use his eyes and ears all the better as he traveled west through Persia to India, then south through Phoenicia and Palestine to Egypt.

"I suppose it was a foolish notion," he said to me once, "but I was young then, and young men are always ready to think in absolutes. I would never have kept the vow had I gone to Egypt before I went to India and there encountered the Gymnosophists—the naked philosophers of the Thebaid. Contemplation of their state cured me of any further wish to take the business of living to its imaginable extremes."

"But you did not begin eating meat," I pointed out to him, "nor wearing animal relics upon your body."

"You could not think that an extreme," he chided me, "were you not a young man, and one who has never known poverty."

As to the reputation that Apollonius had as a healer and an exorcist, I believe that he was as clever as any man of his time—which is to say that the advice he gave to all men who were sick in body was to avoid meat and medicines, and the advice he gave to all men who believed themselves possessed was to avoid meat and magicians. I have offered the same advice throughout my own long life; by my reckoning, it leads to the recovery of three suffers in every five, which is at least one more in five than regain their health after consulting doctors or wizards. Damis, of course, gives a different account—but doubtless he has his reasons.

Which brings us to my own sad case, which Damis calls bewitchment—although I remember it as nothing worse than love-sickness.

* * * * * * *

Apollonius visited Corinth in his sixtieth year, or shortly thereafter. He was welcomed into the household of the Cynic philosopher Demetrius, an avid follower of his doctrines, among whose pupils I was to be counted. I was twenty-five years old, and even Damis concedes that I was handsome and athletic.

Damis misstates the case when he says that I was betrothed to a foreign woman who represented herself as a wealthy Phoenician. I was certainly enamored of a foreign woman, but she was an Egyptian servant named Nauma, a minor adjunct of the household of a Phoenician widow called Galanthis.

Galanthis had been some months a guest in the house of a rich merchant named Aradus, who had known her for many years through her husband, with whom he had had commercial connections. Aradus was the father of Bassus, a man of my own age with whom I had grown up, although some strain had been placed on our friendship by virtue of the fact that he too was inclined to think of himself as a philosopher, although he was an unrepentant hedonist. I used to think of our arguments as a kind of sport but Demetrius took a dimmer view of them and regarded Bassus as a malign influence who threatened his authority over all his pupils.

I must confess that I was by no means the best or most faithful pupil of Demetrius. I had found, while under his tutelage, that I had little heart for the ascetic life towards which Demetrius was continually urging me. Although I recognized that they were mostly excuses for conscienceless self-indulgence, I was not unattracted by the rival doctrines of Bassus. I was firmly committed to the ideals of philosophy, but I was at that time quite uncertain as to which set of ideals was to be preferred. Should it not be possible, I wondered, for a man of wisdom to enjoy life to the full? Should it not be permissible to eat good meat, drink good wine, wear good shoes and love women—marry, even—while still cultivating the art and authority of the mind? Demetrius said that it was not, but Bassus said otherwise.

Such was the antipathy which grew up between Demetrius and Bassus that Bassus became increasingly determined to steal me for his own fledgling school. He might have succeeded in doing so before Apollonius arrived in Corinth, had it not been for the fact that, when I visited the house of Aradus in the month before the fateful visit, time spent with Bassus always seemed to be time that ought to have been spent with Nauma. Paradoxically, it was not until I was well away from the house that the words of Bassus began to exert their grip upon me—by which time Demetrius was usually on hand to refute the arguments in the strongest possible terms.

Quite without meaning to, I became the most significant prize that had ever been put at stake in the war of ideas waged between the two men—and Nauma became involved, in spite of the fact that she had not the slightest interest in philosophy. Her one and only vocation was dancing; Galanthis had acquired her on account of her skill in that art—and, I hasten to add, for her skill in that art alone. Even Damis of Nineveh does not dare to allege—as my master Demetrius sometimes did—that my beloved was no more than a common whore.

"She may be a servant," I told my master, aggrievedly, "but Nauma is far too precious to be sold in that manner."

"Only because Galanthis intends to wed Aradus herself," Demetrius insisted. "She dangles her serving-maids before him as a cunning fisherman displays the lure, but you may be sure that he shall not touch them—yet."

"Bassus says that his father is perfectly content as a widower," I told Demetrius. "He has slave-girls of his own."

"If Bassus says that, it is hope speaking," Demetrius retorted. "He fears for his father's fortune, should the Phoenician ever get her greedy hands upon it, and he has extended his debts to the limit with every moneylender in Corinth. Aradus may be a prince of fools, too long retired from the marketplace, but even he knows better than to pay his son's debts. You may not see what Bassus is, but Aradus does—he knows that an appetite such as that, once unleashed, is likely to devour wealth as a plague of locusts devours a field of green wheat."

It was, indeed, hope rather than faith that determined Bassus' opinion. On the same day that Demetrius was told to expect Apollonius in Corinth, Aradus announced that his betrothal to Galanthis would be marked by a sumptuous feast. This was the "wedding-feast" to which Damis refers in his memoir; it was not mine, although I and my beloved were certainly there—and so was Apollonius.

* * * * * * *

Damis claims that Apollonius used magic to unmask my beloved and expose her as a lamia—a serpentine demon

11

whose intention was to drink my blood and feed on my flesh. He also claims that Apollonius proved that all the gold and silver at the wedding-feast was mere illusion. He did neither of these things, and I am certain in my own mind that he never told Damis exactly what did happen, although Damis seems to have learned more about the matter that he perceived at the time. Apollonius did recognize a serpent, which the other diners could not see, and he did unravel a strange web of illusion in order to assist in the awkward business of my education—but the "magic" he used was no more than memory and philosophy.

My first meeting with Apollonius was not a happy one, for Demetrius was in a very sarcastic mood when he introduced me. "This," he said, "is Menippus. I do not know whether he will be a member of my school much longer, for he dwells in the gardens of Tantalus, fascinated by the luxury of his dear friend Bassus and mesmerized by the allure of an Egyptian temptress, who dances—or so I am told—like a snake bewitched by a charmer's pipe."

I remember that Damis of Nineveh laughed aloud at this. Perhaps that is why he records in his memoir that his master advised me there and then that I was "cherishing a serpent". In fact, Apollonius said no such thing, and looked at me with a certain sympathy when he saw how hurt and embarrassed I was by my master's unkind words.

"It is good that a man should pass through the gardens of Tantalus," Apollonius said. "How else is he to learn that their promise is false, their reward an illusion? There will be time enough to judge Menippus when he has made his own judgment as to the worth of what is dangled before him."

I had a speech of my own prepared. "I met the merchant Aradus yesterday," I told the great sage. "He asked me if the world-renowned Apollonius of Tyana were indeed expected to arrive in Corinth today. When I said that you were, he told me that his dearest wish was that the enmity between his son Bassus and the Cynic Demetrius might be set aside for the day of his betrothal. Aradus would be greatly honored if you and Demetrius would come together to the feast, and give your blessing to the union between himself and Galanthis. He knows that you will not eat meat and do not like finery but he says that there will be fruit and bread a-plenty, and that such finery as he intends to display is not intended as an insult to the poor, but merely as a celebration of his own good fortune. He would dearly like Bassus and Demetrius to be friends again, and he hopes that your benign influence might serve to ease the bitterness between them."

Demetrius scowled, but he dared not make any response until the great man had spoken.

"You may tell Aradus that I will come," Apollonius said, "but you must warn him that I cannot settle other people's quarrels with honeyed words. I am a philosopher, not an envoy of Rome. The purpose of my arguments is to arrive at the truth, not to negotiate settlements."

"I will tell him that," I promised. "He will be very glad that your presence will dignify his betrothal feast."

"So he should be," said Damis of Nineveh—although Apollonius frowned at his impoliteness.

"There is no possibility of any reconciliation between the ideas of Bassus and those of better men," Demetrius said, pointedly. "His answer to the question of how men should live is that they should feed their appetites without restraint; the better answer is that men should become masters of their appetites. Luxury is the greatest barrier to the path of enlightenment."

Demetrius looked to Apollonius for support, and I could see that he expected it; he saw the invitation to the feast of Aradus as one more phase in his battle with Bassus for the prize of my allegiance, and he trusted Apollonius to win the battle for him—but all Apollonius said in reply was: "There is more than one path to enlightenment, and there are many barriers that might blind a man to the truth."

Damis of Nineveh was enthusiastic to lend his support to these words, but I am sure now that he never understood their meaning.

* * * * * * *

The day of the betrothal-feast was beautiful and clear; the most superstitious of men would have searched in vain for any omen of what was to come.

I had never seen such a repast as that which Aradus laid out for his guests, for he had gone to extraordinary lengths to make sure that the day would not be forgotten. Although he was no longer the busy man he had been fifteen years before, he remembered with great fondness the days when he had built up his petty empire. His ships brought abundant cargoes from Antioch, Caesaria, and Alexandria, and carried the best of Corinth's produce to Ancona and to Rome. He had been a man of great influence in his time, and he was still an example to the younger men who followed in his footsteps.

The governor himself, Marcellus Cato, had come to sit at Aradus' right hand. He had his doctor and his astrologer in close attendance, and a dozen men-at-arms under the immediate command of a centurion named Calidius. Arrayed below the governor's party were the wealthiest men in Corinth, landowners and merchants alike. They were men whose names were known to everyone: the men who determined the commerce of Corinth. Almost without exception, they were accompanied by the sons and nephews who would one day inherit their wealth and their concerns. They were so many that the position left to mere philosophers—even to philosophers as famous as Apollonius of Tyana—was a long way down the line, but Apollonius made no objection to his placing and Demetrius swallowed his pride.

When we sat down, Damis of Nineveh made as if to take the place at his master's left, but the sage asked him to sit to the right of Demetrius, and gave me the place Damis had tried to claim. He asked me to put names to the people in the crowd, and I did so, adding further information when I thought it relevant—which compelled me to whisper in his ear, for some of the things I said were best not overheard.

"The governor is a bitter man," I told him, "but not unreasonable. I know that Corinth does not rank as high in Roman estimation as its citizens think it should, and Marcellus Cato considers it a place of exile—far better, no doubt, than some tiny island in the Aegean, but no fit place for a nobleman. He was a friend of Nero, but fell from favor when Nero died, and was sent here by Vespasian. He has been awaiting his recall ever since Vespasian's death, but that was seven years ago and it seems that the time may never come."

14

"Such is the fate of most of Nero's friends," Apollonius observed. "He was emperor when I was in Rome, but he did not like me and I did not stay long. My tastes were too austere for him, my philosophy too sparse. He might have preferred your friend Bassus."

"Bassus affects to despise Rome," I told him, in a diplomatic whisper. "Even a man as fond of Greek ways as Nero would not meet his approval. Aradus is always lavish in his praise for the Empire, but I think he conceals his real opinion."

"There is still a tendency in Greece to think of the Romans as barbarians," Apollonius agreed. "It is true that they have followed where Alexander led—but it is also true that they have held what Alexander lost."

Having been seated at his right hand I could not help but try to see the feast as I imagined Apollonius saw it, through austere and forbidding eyes. The luxury of it might have seemed an unalloyed marvel, had he not been there beside me, but in his presence I felt a creeping unease about its extravagance.

Galanthis was magnificently dressed in silks and golden threads, but with Apollonius beside me I could not help but see that the powders and paints with which she made up her face were masking wrinkles and flesh made soft by an indulgent life. She smiled a great deal, but my impression was that her smiles were forced, and that some dire anxiety was lurking beneath her good humor. Poor Bassus did not even bother to smile. Everyone knew that he did not want the wedding to take place, for fear that Aradus would alter his will, diverting a too-substantial part of his wealth to his new bride. Perhaps there was nothing to be gained by his pretending to enjoy himself, but I could not help but think that he was being unnecessarily churlish.

Even the food that I tasted was a little spoiled, by virtue of the fact that Apollonius hardly ate at all. The plate that had been set before him remained empty and his knife lay idle. He took what he needed between his fingers, one patient morsel at a time. I was not so deeply entranced by him that I neglected to try the dishes I had never seen before, but every time I filled my mouth I felt disappointed; it was, after all, only food—and even the best of the taste-sensations I had not previously experienced were not unusually pleasant. There was an astonishing profusion of sweetmeats, decked out in many colors and formed into many shapes—but their sweetness was, after all only honey or beet-sugar, and the ones most cunningly wrought had been so hardened in the cooking as to endanger the teeth of anyone trying to bite into one.

"You might try one of these," I said to Apollonius, who had finished eating long before I had sampled everything that intrigued me, and had begun to make me feel uncomfortable. "The sticky centre is like the essence of an orange—but you must suck the outer part patiently until it dissolves; there is no short cut."

"Thank you, Menippus," said the sage, "but I find all such confections overly sickly. Is that the dancing girl of whom your master disapproves so strongly?"

It was indeed my beloved Nauma, decked out in all her finery as I had never seen her before, ready to play her part in the evening's entertainment. She jangled as she danced, for her silks were sown with hundreds of little silver coins.

The tables set out for the feast were arranged in the form of an inverted U, so Nauma danced at first in the space between the twin ends of the base, but she slowly made her way up the ranks, crossing the distance between the two limbs again and again. I had seen her dance a dozen times before, in public and in private, but this was an occasion like no other and this was a dance like no other. One still hears people speak of the Judean Salomé, who beguiled her stepfather Herod and asked for the head of some petty prophet as a tribute, but I cannot imagine that she danced more delicately or more entrancingly than Nauma danced at the betrothal-feast of Aradus and Galanthis. I had not realized how noisy the room had been until she stilled the noise, claiming a pause for the sound of the lyres and tabors which played for her, and for the magic of her movements.

I do not hesitate, in this instance, to use the word "magic". If there was any magic at the feast, it was certainly hers and hers alone. If there was any spell cast, it was she who cast it—but she cast it with the suppleness of her young limbs and the sinuousness of her lovely body, and the discipline of arduous training. When I saw her dance, I knew exactly why I loved her so dearly—and why every man in that great pavilion had cause to envy me.

A snake bewitched by a charmer's pipe, Demetrius had said—but she was not that. Perhaps there was something in her swaying reminiscent of the flow of a serpent's body, and something in her silks and silver trimmings that recalled the sparkle of sunlight on a serpent's scales, but there was so much more. Nauma had arms and legs, hands and feet, full lips and glorious eyes. She was a human being, through and through. Even looking at her, as I was forced to do, in the knowledge that the ascetic Apollonius was sitting beside me, I lost myself in rapt contemplation of her beauty. I am sure that others did likewise, although I saw that some few of the merchants were distracted by the coins, which she now began to release from her costume and scatter about the top of the table.

I might have found an unalloyed joy in Nauma's performance had it not been that, when she finally reached the climax of her dance, she threw herself across the table, planting her painted lips upon the mouth of the astonished Aradus in evident tribute. I could not suppress a horrid shock of jealous rage as I saw him overcome his surprise in time to take full advantage of the kiss, pressing his lips avidly to hers. It was, I suppose, the kind of lascivious act that a man might be forgiven at his betrothal feast, but I could not help but remember what Demetrius had said to me about the cunning fisherman, and how Galanthis was using her delectable slave-girls as bait to entrap her groom.

For a moment, I did indeed see the wedding-feast as the gardens of Tantalus, promising so much but without any real substance—but then I remembered that that was exactly how Demetrius wanted me to see it, in order that I might remain a Cynic like himself forever, and I wondered whether that was what I really wanted to be. I looked along the length of the tables, towards the high place where Bassus sat, but I could not catch his eye. He too was absorbed in watching Nauma, who had withdrawn from the embrace of Aradus to take her bow.

The noise returned explosively as the company burst out clapping and cheering. I looked back at Aradus, and saw that he was beating the table with his huge right hand. His mouth was closed, but there was an expression on his face that seemed close to bliss. I could not bear it, and turned to face Apollonius.

"No doubt you have seen such dances before, in the course of your travels," I said to him, taking care to keep my voice level.

"In Egypt," he said, "and in India too—but not in Rome. Nero had little more taste for pretty dancing girls than your master has." I could not judge the exact quality of his tone, but it seemed to have mellowed just a little. I studied his face, wondering whether a man of his great age could still be stirred in the loins, or whether he merely remembered a time when he might have reacted more passionately—but then the noise about the table changed again, transformed in an instant from wild applause into horror.

It was not until the centurion raced forward to take control that I realized what had happened. Calidius had to draw his sword in order to clear a space, so that his men might come forward and take up the still-writhing body of the stricken Aradus. They carried him away into the house, with Marcellus Cato's doctor in hot pursuit.

* * * * * * *

Had the death of Aradus happened on any other day I would have been cast adrift on the sea of rumor, with no more opportunity to discover what had happened than any gossiping slave. I might never have discovered the truth. But this was the day that Apollonius of Tyana had come to Corinth, and Apollonius had the reputation of being a healer without equal. Within a quarter of an hour Marcellus Cato had sent a messenger to the sage, imploring him to render what assistance he could to his own doctor; because I was still at Apollonius' side, I went with him, along with Demetrius and Damis.

Damis and I were not allowed to go to the crowded bedside, so I had no opportunity to see what condition Aradus was in, but when Demetrius came out again into the ante-chamber I knew that the matter was very grave.

"He is dying," Demetrius said. "No healer in the world could save him."

"Do not underestimate my master," Damis said. "I have seen him work wonders."

Demetrius shook his head. "The man has suffered some kind of fit," he said. "He was overexcited by the sight of that accursed girl, inflamed by her lewd dancing. You saw how avidly he returned her kiss. There is a lesson in this, Menippus!"

I was hurt that he should try to make argumentative capital out of such a misfortune, but I had no time to reply. Bassus came hurtling from the room then, his face contorted with fury. He stopped as soon as he saw me—but I think he would have stopped for anyone who might give him a hearing.

"Sorcery!" he said. "Vile sorcery has killed him! That enchantress is behind it, I swear. She has killed my father! Menippus, you must help me drive her out of Corinth."

I took this speech as an expression of grief. Bassus had never seemed overly fond of his surviving parent, but a father is, after all, a father. I could not imagine that Galanthis had any reason for wanting to slay the man she had been on the point of marrying, nor was I prepared to entertain the possibility that she was a sorceress who could strike a man down with a curse, but my first impulse was to soothe my friend's distress. I went to embrace him, hoping to calm his wrath, but Demetrius caught me by the shoulder.

"Stay!" my master said. "Clearly, the man is mad."

"Mad he is!" The new voice came from the doorway of the bedroom, and I knew it was Galanthis before I turned to look. She waited until we were all staring at her before she continued. "There is only one man here who had motive for murder," she declared, "and there he stands." She was pointing a long-nailed finger at Bassus. "He feared the loss of all his expectations, and he made haste to strike—to deny the father who patiently bore the burden of his every excess a few lost years of happiness. Murderer! Parricide!"

What Bassus had said had astonished me, but this tirade left me thunderstruck. I could not believe that the Phoenician meant her accusations seriously, and imagined that they had been provoked by an ugly combination of grief and wrath—grief at the death of her intended spouse and wrath occasioned by his wild talk of sorcery.

Just as I had moved towards Bassus, Demetrius and Damis moved towards Galanthis. They did not embrace her but she took their movement for approval. "See!" she said to Bassus. "They know what you are! Everyone shall know it!"

In his memoir, which separates the incident from the wrongly-attributed betrothal-feast, Damis says that Apollonius argued with Bassus and called him parricide, but it was Damis and Demetrius who stood with the angry Phoenician and supported her words with their stares, while I clung hard to Bassus, making sure that he could not react violently to the slander. Demetrius met my eyes, and I could tell that he was instructing me to consider carefully what company I was keeping, but it was Damis who opened his mouth to speak and his manner suggested that he was not about to play the peacemaker.

What Damis would have said only Damis knows, and I suspect that the accusations he now credits to Apollonius were the product of a later fancy. At the time, he was silenced by the entry of Marcellus Cato, who pushed past Galanthis to take a stand between the two accusers. "Be silent!" he commanded them both. "It is my place to discover whether any murder has been done, and my place to determine the responsibility. Are you mad, both of you? Whatever you think or feel, at least be quiet while the poor man lies upon his bed, fighting for his life."

Bassus' reaction to this instruction was to throw up his hands and turn on his heel. He marched off, not bothering to look at me again, let alone invite me to follow. I could not help thinking that it was not the behavior expected of a philosopher, nor even of a man of common sense.

"A man should be master of his feelings," murmured Demetrius, unable to resist the temptation, "not their slave." His eyes were still fixed on me, and for once I had no reply. I looked at the ground between my feet.

Galanthis hesitated for a moment, but then she went back into the bedchamber, presumably to wait by the bedside of her husband-to-be. The governor followed her. I heard no more voices raised in anger within the chamber—merely a low hum of whispered discussion.

"My master will know the truth," Damis said, loftily. "Nothing escapes him, though lesser men are oft deluded." He named no "lesser men" but it was obvious that distaste for Roman upstarts was not confined to Greece. I considered the possibility that the men of Nineveh and Babylon—whose empire had fallen to Alexander as Alexander's had fallen to Rome—might see Greeks and Romans in much the same harsh light.

Eventually, Apollonius came out, accompanied by the governor's doctor and astrologer. Marcellus Cato and Calidius followed two or three paces behind, with the steward of the household.

"It was a natural fit," the doctor opined, "brought on by age and excitement."

"I am not so sure," the astrologer said. "There might indeed be sorcery at work here. I can sense its presence."

The governor, who seemed to be well used to such disagreements, sighed in exasperation. "What do you say, Cappadocian?" he asked Apollonius.

"I have seen the symptoms before," Apollonius replied, equably. "When a man has a reputation as a healer, he is forever being summoned to the sick and dying, and he learns to read the signs. This is a puzzling case, in that I have never seen the signs so dire, but I can say with certainty that no sorcery was involved."

"Nor was any poison," said the steward, quickly. He was so anxious to avoid questions being asked regarding his own areas of responsibility that he did not wait to see whether anyone would raise the question.

"Certainly not," Marcellus Cato was quick to say. He had been sitting beside the stricken man, taking his food from the same plates and pouring his wine from the same flasks.

"The food was tasted," Calidius growled. "Wherever a Roman governor comes to eat, the food is tasted—even in

Corinth." The tone of his voice implied, unjustly, that Corinth was no safer than Damascus or Castra Regina.

"I smell sorcery," said the astrologer, still smarting beneath Apollonius' contradiction. "No matter what the Cappadocian says...."

"Utter nonsense," said the doctor. "A natural fit. The man had cultivated his pleasures excessively. Long overindulgence in food and wine leads in the end to an exhaustion of the flesh." He glanced at Apollonius as he said this, obviously expecting approval. The sage said nothing, although Demetrius nodded his head vigorously.

The governor was still looking at Apollonius. "Is that true, Master Philosopher?" he said. "Was it the merchant's way of life that determined the manner of his death?"

For the merest instant, I thought I saw the ghost of a smile hovering upon the sage's lips. "I believe you have stated the case exactly, sir," he said.

The governor bowed his head in acknowledgement of the compliment. "In the absence of evidence to the contrary," he said, glancing at his astrologer as he stressed the word *evidence*, "it seems to me that this is a clear case of death by natural causes. When the son and the wife-to-be have calmed down, I will hear what they have to say—but if they wish to bring forward any accusations that would make this sad affair the business of Rome, they had better have proof, for I will tolerate no baseless slanders." His gaze flickered back and forth, from the astrologer to the doctor to the steward, then from Apollonius to Demetrius to Calidius, and finally from Damis to me. He knew that what he said would be reported back to Bassus, and what he said was intended to be thus reported. In a quieter voice, speaking to Apollonius alone, the governor added: "You had better go now, Master Philosopher."

Apollonius nodded, and allowed Demetrius to lead him away. I followed, with Damis of Nineveh.

* * * * * * *

Apollonius was not called to give any further testimony in the case. Bassus made no further accusations against Galanthis, nor she against him, but that did not stop the rumors. Whatever barriers there are to enlightenment, there are none to vile whispers.

Word flew to the city walls and beyond, saying that Aradus had been murdered by sorcery or poison, and that Bassus had done it to make sure of his inheritance. It transpired that the will of Aradus had not been changed to the disadvantage of Bassus, although the dead man had left behind a letter requesting that Bassus should treat Galanthis generously, and this revelation added fuel to the speculation. The fact that Galanthis accepted the situation was construed as evidence that he had bought her silence, and the more ingenious rumor-mongers went so far as to wonder whether the two of them had conspired together to cause the death of Aradus, because they were secret lovers impatient to acquire his wealth.

Throughout the next two days I was pestered by people who knew that I had been with Apollonius when he had been summoned to Aradus' bedside. I soon became impatient with them, because I had troubles of my own, whose pressure on my heart and mind increased inexorably. My first thought, after quitting the company of Demetrius and Apollonius, had been to find Nauma and see how she was faring—but she was nowhere to be found. The house of Aradus was in such confusion that it was not easy to pursue my search, and I was eventually persuaded to leave it for the morrow, but when I went back again, and still found no trace of her, I became very anxious.

Galanthis said that she did not know where Nauma was, and did not seem to care. None of the Phoenician's other servants had seen her go, or knew of anywhere she might have gone. I could not believe that she had left the city without even pausing to say goodbye to me, but there was no trace of her within its walls.

It was a mystery—far more of a mystery, so far as I was concerned, than the death of Aradus. It seemed obvious to me that the two events were connected somehow, and it seemed so to the rumor-mongers too, who quickly began to speculate that Nauma had been the instrument of Bassus and Galanthis, and had been sent away lest she tell what she

knew. I was sure that this was untrue, because Bassus swore
to me that he had no knowledge whatsoever of the girl's
whereabouts, but I was sorely confused as to what the real
situation might be.

In the end, I decided to take my problem to Apollonius.
I felt, however, that I had to speak to him alone, for I knew
that Demetrius would certainly be angry with me and I suspected that Damis would laugh at me. While I awaited my
opportunity I tried to look at the matter as he would undoubtedly look at it, through the eyes of a philosopher, so
that I would not seem too much of a fool when I laid it out
before him.

* * * * * * *

Night had fallen, for the second time since the betrothal
feast, by the time I finally found the chance to be alone with
Apollonius. Demetrius and Damis had gone to their beds,
and so had everyone else—even Cynics need sleep, but
Apollonius, it seemed, had progressed beyond mere Cynicism to some further realm of mental existence.

"I need the benefit of your wisdom," I told him.

"Perhaps you do," he agreed. "Come walk with me, and
we shall see what benefit we can derive from careful discussion."

We walked together in the moonlight, up the hill that
stands above the southern quarter of the town. We paused on
a ridge, from which we could look back over the rooftops,
towards the quays where the merchants' ships loaded and
unloaded their goods. While we went I told him everything—not merely that Nauma had disappeared, but *everything*. I told him how I felt about her, and how it had weak-
ened my faith in the doctrines of Demetrius and forced me to
take the ideas of Bassus more seriously than before. I told
him that I could not see why philosophers could not live like
other men, rather than in retreat from society, or why they
did better not to marry. I told him that I could not see why
love was such a threat to the philosophical calmness of mind,
although I was beginning to understand that the passions
aroused by its loss might blot out the capacity for reason.

24

"Your reason does not seem to me to have been entirely blotted out," Apollonius said. "Tell me, Menippus, what is it that you fear most? Is it the possibility that you may never see your lovely dancer again, or the possibility that she might not have been what you supposed?"

I paused to consider that question carefully, knowing that my answer would determine what he thought of me. In the end, I said: "What I fear most is that she might have been murdered, to prevent her telling what she knew about the death of Aradus." I knew it was a risk, but I had carefully thought over what Apollonius had said when he was asked to judge the cause of the merchants' death—and I remembered the ghost of a smile that had haunted his final statement.

"Ah!" he said. "I doubt that you need fear that. Would you really rather think that she is alive, but does not care about you? Many men, I suspect, would rather think that she had loved them so dearly that only death could keep her from them."

"I would rather she were alive," I said. I hope that I was telling the truth. "I would rather that were so, even if it meant that she was only amusing herself with me until the time came to do what she had to do."

"And what do you think she did?" he asked me, although he knew as well as I did.

I was unable to look him in the eye, but I answered him. "When she kissed Aradus at the conclusion of her dance," I said, slowly, "something passed from her mouth to his. He did not open his mouth to cheer, you see, when she had finished, although he pounded the table with all his might. It was one of those sweetmeats, I suppose. The poison was hidden inside a hard sugary coat, unreleased until he had sucked it through."

Apollonius said nothing in reply to that. He looked out over the city of Corinth as if he were weighing it in the balance—not merely the city but everything it signified: its history; its commerce; its role in the affairs of empire.

"What kind of poison was it?" I asked him, delicately.

"I had seen the symptoms before," he said, eventually. "Always in association with the bite of a snake—usually the

Egyptian cobra. In Alexandria they call it Cleopatra's last lover."

"The asp," I said, to demonstrate that I had knowledge of my own.

"What puzzled me when I attended Aradus," Apollonius went on, "is that the bite of the asp is very rarely fatal, in my experience. Whatever they may say about Cleopatra, I have never seen anyone but a small child die of a cobra bite. In India they have much bigger snakes called hamadryads, whose bite is said to be far more deadly, but I saw snake-charmers in India who had little or no fear of the creatures they employed. It's not easy to know which rumors are to be trusted and which are not, is it, Menippus?"

It did not seem necessary to confirm my agreement with that judgment.

"Surely she cannot have known what she was doing," I said, "Else she'd never have allowed such a treacherous thing into her mouth. If she was ordered to do it by her mistress, why? If she was paid to do it, by whom? And how was the poison obtained? There is no cobra nearer than Persia or Palestine."

"I watched the snake-charmers of India most carefully," Apollonius told me. "They would not have told me their secret, of course, even if I had not been silent at the time, so I felt that I had to find it out. I made a game of it—I made games of many such quests while I was clinging to my silly vow. At first I thought that they were simply quick enough to avoid the strikes of their playthings—there are creatures call mongooses which kill cobras easily enough by means of their agility. Then I wondered whether the charmers might build up a tolerance to the bites. In the end, I caught one unawares while he was preparing his toys. He was milking its venom into a wooden cup, extracting the creature's entire supply of poison. He had five snakes in all; I imagine that he built up a concentration of venom far greater than any ordinary bite was likely to communicate. He simply threw it away—I thought at the time that it was profligate, that such a commodity might be saleable. Perhaps it can be stored indefinitely in a vial, or preserved in some sticky syrup like the

26

one in the centre of one of those horrible sweetmeats you urged me to try."

The sweetmeats had not seemed horrible to me while I sucked them at the feast—but they have always seemed so since I talked to Apollonius.

"Who gave it to her?" I wanted to know. "Was it Galanthis?"

"Galanthis had nothing to gain," Apollonius said. "She is dependent on the generosity of Bassus now—and you know better than I what that is worth."

"Bassus, then?" I whispered. "Can he really have been so desperate?"

"You know better than I," Apollonius repeated.

"I don't believe it," I said. "In any case, had he been minded to put his father away he'd never have chosen such a method and he'd have found a far more convenient time. But who, then?"

"Who is left?" he parried.

I still remembered the ghost of his smile. He had already delivered his verdict: it was the manner in which Aradus had lived his life that had determined the manner of his death.

"Marcellus Cato?" I suggested. "Is it possible that the governor murdered Aradus? Is that why you said nothing when he declared that no murder had been committed? Did you think he would strike you down if you denounced him?"

"I think he recognized the hand of his masters, as I did," Apollonius said. "Perhaps he was meant to. There are those in Rome who reckon that it is always a good idea to remind dissatisfied exiles that they have not been forgotten. Calidius is a more likely assassin. It was he who fetched me to see the body, he who studied me most carefully as I made my replies. I think we understood one another well enough, Calidius and I. I am an ancient philosopher, he is an ambitious centurion—we have no reason to quarrel. The likelihood is that he and the girl were working in collusion. You must hope so, if you told me the truth. A mere pawn would be dead by now, but not a skilled executioner whose services would soon be needed elsewhere."

I thought about those possibilities for a minute or two before moving on to the next question. "Why?" I asked. "Why should Rome want Aradus dead?"

"I'm a philosopher," Apollonius said, "not an oracle. I can only guess."

I did not need to tell him that I rated a philosopher's guesses far more highly than an oracle's pronouncements. I simply said: "Go on."

"We must consider the time and the place," he said. "Assassins usually work by night, brutally and secretly. When they work by day, it is because they have a point to make. If Cato might have been expected to find a message in the incident, so might others. This was not merely a murder; it was the interruption of a feast celebrating the betrothal of two people long connected by their business. Did you look closely at any of those coins the dancer let fall?"

"No," I admitted.

"I have never used money," Apollonius said. "It has always been a point of pride—but perhaps it was also a stubborn refusal to submit to temptation. Money is so fascinating, is it not? Such a wonderful invention. Whatever tales we tell of the military genius of Alexander, the true heart of the Greek empire was coin. Before Athens, all cities grew their own food in their own fields; Athens was the first to obtain its food by trade, putting its artisans to work in the manufacture of goods for the marketplace, and it was *money* that made the marketplace possible. For four centuries after Solon, it is said, the Athenian drachma held its real value: sixty-seven grains of silver before Alexander, sixty-five thereafter—and then came Rome. The *denarius* held its real value while Augustus was emperor, but Tiberius and Claudius began the debasement that Nero completed. Now, the value of a coin is determined by the authority of the emperor whose head is stamped upon it rather than by the value of the metal it contains. Anyone with the skill to make alloys and a crude stamp can increase the supposed value of their metal four- or five-fold by making an image of the emperor. Small wonder that they do—and small wonder that the Romans resent that kind of usurpation. They think of forgery as the rot that might eat away their empire from within, refusing

28

to admit that the real rot is the pretence that an emperor's authority can sustain more value in a coin than it would have in ordinary barter."

I did not know for sure that Aradus had been a forger, or a dealer in false coin, but I knew that it was more than likely. Corinth lay on the trade routes linking Rome to the east, to lands that resented Roman dominion even more than Greece. It was common knowledge that, since Nero had debased the coinage so dramatically, every metalworker in Asia Minor was seeking to take advantage of the excessive purchasing power of their stocks-in-trade. Every merchant at the top table had probably taken a hand in such dealings—and Marcellus Cato too.

"All that glisters is not gold," I murmured, "and all that sparkles is not silver." I did not mean it literally, and Apollonius knew it.

"I dare say that she liked you well enough," he said, softly. "You're a handsome youth, after all—but she always knew that you were a philosopher. You *are* a philosopher, Menippus, no matter what Demetrius may think—and there are more paths than one to enlightenment, and more ways than one to cross the barriers that block the way. Be a Cynic by all means, but be a realist too. Love if you can; marry if you must—but choose your lovers and your wife with the same care you'd use in choosing a philosophy. There's a good deal of false coin in every marketplace in the world, and I doubt that the world will ever see the end of it now that it's begun."

He was still staring over the rooftops at the distant quays.

"They say that Corinth was a great city," I reflected, "before the Romans came...." I didn't bother to finish the sentence. All cities had been great before the Romans came, just as all merchants had been honest and all pigs had had wings.

Apollonius said nothing more. He waited for me to move on, and I did. I led the way back down the hill, thinking about murder and justice and love. I didn't ask Apollonius why he hadn't declared that Aradus had been murdered, preferring to let his scrupulously truthful words be misinter-

preted and misused. It wasn't that he was scared of retribu-
tion; it was because he was a philosopher. Rome was the
murderer and false money the motive; Rome was also the
law and the falsifier of the money. Apollonius stood aside
from all of that; the truth he sought was a higher and finer
kind.

"A man does not have to be as self-denying as you are
in order to cultivate wisdom," I told him, defensively. I
meant every word, but I was amazed by my own temerity in
framing it as a positive statement rather than a cringing question. "There is room even in a wise man's heart for a little
lust and a little comfort."

"Perhaps there is," he answered. "I purged myself so
ruthlessly in the fever of my youth that I could not recover
any such impulse if I tried, but you might find a better way.
At any rate, you must find your own way. By all means learn
all you can from Demetrius and Bassus, but in the end it is
yourself that you must know, yourself that you must make,
yourself that you must prove."

I knew that. I know it still, and I am not dissatisfied with
what I am. I would not want to be a magician or a prophet,
even in an Age of Miracle-Workers.

"I do love her," I told him, as we parted. "I fear that,
without her love, I'll never be as good a man as I might have
been."

"She might return, in time," Apollonius said, more
kindly than I deserved. "If she loves you, she'll come back."

She never did, of course.

*[Author's note: The only account of the life of Apollonius of
Tyana to have survived into modern times is that written by
Philostratus in the third century A.D. This was allegedly
based on memoirs compiled by Damis of Nineveh, a disciple
and companion of Apollonius, although some commentators
have suspected that these never existed, Philostratus having
invented them to lend weight to his rather fanciful account.
The statements and opinions attributed by Menippus to
Damis in the story are, of course, all derived from Philostratus.]*

THE LOST ROMANCE

[An anonymous tale recorded in Welsh by an unknown hand, circa 1380, here translated into English for the first time by Dafydd V. Evans, Ph.D., edited by Brian Stableford]

I had this tale from a cousin in Chepstow, who had it in his turn from a Cistercian monk who had formerly been the confessor of Brother Simon, the scribe whose adventure it was. Given that it is little more than thirty years old, and that the tellers entrusted with it were undoubtedly honest, you may be sure that every word of it is true.

At the time of his journey, which took place in the Year of Our Lord 1348, Brother Simon was a young man of some twenty-one years. He had been given to the Cistercians at Valle Crucis nine years before and was highly valued by them on two counts. The first was his voice, which retained its melodic loveliness even after it had broken; the second was his intellect, which made him very quick with languages and letters. By virtue of the latter quality he was trained by the order as a scribe, whose principal duty it was to copy the manuscripts held in trust by the Abbey. These manuscripts included, in addition to the Holy Scriptures, a number of parchment scrolls, which had been lodged there by the Abbey's founder, Madoc of Griffith Maellor, who was Lord of Bromfield and was acknowledged by some as Prince of Powis.

The texts comprising Madoc's bequest were written in French and Welsh rather than the Latin of the Church, but it so happened that Simon's father was descended from one of the captains who fought with William the Bastard at Hastings and his mother hailed from Carmarthen. By virtue of this mixed parentage he was fluent in both tongues, and could read as well in either as in Latin. Although many an Abbot would not have considered manuscripts written in vulgar tongues fit for copying, the Superior of Valle Crucis—who was nobly born, and knew French far better than English—had Simon read the French scripts aloud to him, so that he might discover whether there was anything therein worth preserving.

As it happened, the French texts included a prose version of Robert de Borron's poem *Joseph d'Arimathie*, which told the tale of how the cup used by Christ at the Last Supper was employed to catch the blood of his wounds as he hung upon the cross, how that cup was then brought to Britain, and how it subsequently came to be the concern of King Arthur's knights. This the Superior commanded Simon to copy, as a valuable lesson for the education of Christian Britain.

When Simon told the Superior that one of the Welsh scripts also concerned the Holy Grail the Abbot—who had a low opinion of his immediate neighbors—was at first uninterested. When Simon persisted, telling the Abbot that the text told of the actual fate of the grail and of its eventual hiding-place at Cockayne in the county of York, the grizzled Norman dismissed the tale as a crude Welsh lie, but he seemed interested in spite of himself.

"You doubtless have good reasons for your estimation of the Welsh, my lord Abbot," Simon said judiciously, although he had no sympathy at all for the Abbot's prejudice against his mother's people, "but while there is the slightest possibility that the tale might harbor a grain of truth, it must warrant preservation. Even if there is no truth in it at all, it might still do the Lord's work, in teasing its hearers with the notion that the grail still exists, though hidden, and might yet be found by a man sufficiently pure in heart. If I am not set to copy it, it will surely be lost forever, for the ink in which it was inscribed was very poorly concocted, and the ill-cured parchment is rotting away even as we speak."

The Abbot eventually agreed to have the text copied.

At that time, neither the Abbot nor Simon knew whether there actually was a place called Cockayne in the county of York, but, having agreed to the copying, the Abbot of Valle Crucis wrote to the Abbot of Rievaulx to make enquiries.

The Abbot of Rievaulx confirmed that there was indeed a village called Cockayne in the North York Moors, and expressed a strong interest in seeing the text, insisting, furthermore, that it must not be the copied version.

Because Rievaulx was the mother church of the mission established by Saint Bernard, and because the Abbot of Rievaulx was a cousin of the Harding family, he held a higher position in the order than the Abbot of Valle Crucis. Simon's Superior had no alternative but to keep the copy Simon had made and send the original to Yorkshire—and he had also to send Simon along with it, so that he might translate its contents for the Abbot of Rievaulx.

* * * * * * *

We live in happier times nowadays, but in our grandfathers' day there were three times as many people living in England as there are now and the land was less productive, because the *carruca* was by no means as widely used for tillage, as it is today. As your grandfathers will tell you, if any survive, the whole nation was awash with brigands and bandits in those days, and it would have been a very fortunate man who could travel all the way from Valle Crucis to York without encountering at least a few.

Simon was not a fortunate man, although he might have counted himself lucky to get as far as he did without running into trouble, and luckier still to escape with his life.

By the time he came within two days' ride of Selby, Simon had traveled nearly three hundred miles, but the journey had taken him a mere fifty-seven days because there had always been fellow-travelers willing to let him ride on their carts. He had shared space with cabbages and turnips, pigs and fowl, fodder and bones, but on the day he encountered the outlaw band he had been so privileged as to be given a place in a carriage which was taking a gentleman named Richard Shreve from Nottingham to York.

Master Shreve was, of course, accompanied by four servants on horseback as well as the driver of the carriage, but the servants very prudently ran off when the twelve-strong band of brigands made its appearance and stopped the carriage. A charitable man might assume that their guiding impulse was to save their master's coursers from being looted along with his carriage-horses.

Master Shreve, on the other hand, drew his sword as soon as the carriage was stopped and leapt boldly down. He offered to meet any one of the marauders in a fair fight, but while he was blustering away at the green-clad man of dark complexion who was evidently the leader of the robber band, one of the brigands slipped around behind him and bludgeoned him to the ground.

While the man with the cudgel was relieving Master Shreve of his pouch, the outlaw chief addressed himself to the driver and the monk. "I beg you to note," he said in English, "that I could easily have killed this reckless fool, but had him knocked on the noggin instead. He'll wake within the hour, none the worse. I wish you to note, also, that I did not instruct my men to fire arrows after his servants, even though I might have enriched myself to the tune of four more horses had my cunning marksmen contrived to bring the riders down. Nor shall I harm a hair on the head of either one of you, provided only that you play fair with me and surrender your possessions peacefully. All I ask in return is that you should tell anyone who asks that Reuben the Jew is the gentlest of all the brigands in England, and a man of honor after his own unorthodox fashion."

The coach-driver grudgingly gave up his own purse, which contained but a few copper coins, and a ring from his finger—and then, after some further persuasion, took off his coat and boots.

"I fear that I have nothing to surrender," Brother Simon said. "Neither coin nor ornament." It was, of course, plain to see that he had no coat to cover his habit, and nothing on his feet but sandals.

"What's that in the satchel?" the outlaw chief demanded.

"Merely a manuscript," the monk replied, "which I am commissioned to carry to the Abbot of Rievaulx."

"Give it to me," the brigand demanded, dismounting from his horse.

Brother Simon handed the satchel over to him.

34

"What language is this?" asked the brigand, as soon as he had unrolled the parchment. "Not Latin or Hebrew, that's for sure."

"Welsh," said Brother Simon.

"What use is a manuscript writ in Welsh?" said the robber, sneeringly.

"As much use as any writ in Latin," Simon retorted, although it was far from clear that his opinion would coincide with the judgment of the Church, "to those who can read it."

The brigand laughed. "I've met the Abbot of Rievaulx," he said. "I once had the pleasure of robbing him, and a very tidy haul he provided. He could barely speak English, let alone Welsh—and although my French is as good as any man's, I never use it. That's for the sake of my loyal followers, who are English through and through."

"Nevertheless," Simon replied, stubbornly, "the Abbot of Rievaulx has asked to see the manuscript and it is my duty to convey it to him. I shall translate the tale for him, if God will see me safely to my destination."

"A tale, is it?" said the outlaw. "What kind of tale, pray tell?"

"It tells of the cup that caught Christ's blood on Calvary," Simon said, "and how it was brought to England by Joseph of Arimathea."

"Oh, *that* tale," said the outlaw, in a tone of frank disgust. "Flowery French rubbish, glorifying the exploits of petty barons and their hired thugs, pretending that they were honest and chaste, and engaged in God's good work rather than the brutal oppression of common folk for the sake of their own enrichment. Chrétien de Troyes and his lying kin have much to answer for. Such stuff would be hateful to every honest British man, if only he could look beyond the studied piety to see the vile truth."

"That is not so," said Simon, boldly. "Arthur was a British king, and the knights he sent in search of the Grail were British too. Arthur was neither Norman nor Saxon, and had not a drop of Viking blood within him—he was a Welshman by blood and by instinct, and his knights were probably Welsh too, no matter how the Norman poets have chosen to rename them. This tale—and others I have seen, similarly written in Welsh—make it abundantly clear that Britain is the true home of chivalry."

There was some restlessness among the outlaws now, and for a moment Simon thought that his brave words had either disturbed or enthused them—but then he realized that they were simply impatient to be on their way lest Master Shreve's servants should have summoned help. They did not approve of their leader pausing to argue about the substance of romances with a monk who had nothing worth stealing.

"Yes, lads," said the robber chief, "you're right. But I haven't quite finished with this lad and I want him brought along. John, you must ride bareback on one of those horses taken from the carriage, for I doubt that a monk has the skill to ride without a saddle."

The man addressed as John protested at this, not relishing the idea of being put up on a carthorse, but his legs were uncommonly long and the animal's great girth posed no real problem to him. When he walked past the fallen body of Richard Shreve, however, the fallen gentleman grabbed his ankle and tripped him up. Shreve was conscious, but very befuddled, and his sword had been taken away, so he posed no real danger to anyone, but when John got up again he hauled the man unceremoniously to his feet and made as if to smash a meaty fist into the neatly-shaven face.

"No!" said the outlaw chief. "I said that I wouldn't harm the man and I meant it. Set him up before you on the carthorse and bring him along—he and his bookish friend shall both be our guests for supper."

John scowled more fiercely than before, but he obeyed. He and Richard Shreve set themselves on the bare back of the carthorse, with the bigger man's arms enfolding the torso of the smaller as they grasped an improvised rein. Simon was given a saddled horse and allowed to ride freely—but the outlaw chief still had his satchel and his manuscript, so he had no alternative but to follow meekly where the outlaws led.

The bootless coachman was left to his own devices, to make his way to Selby in his own good time.

* * * * * * *

The outlaw band rode through forest and field for some three miles before arriving at an isolated cottage on the edge of a wood. It had no stable, but the horses were put away in a barn a hundred yards away and half the outlaws stayed with them. The chief and his remaining half dozen men took Richard Shreve and Brother Simon indoors, where there was a good fire burning, with a huge cooking pot set on top of it.

Simon had noticed a vegetable garden behind the cottage and he did not doubt that the outlaws were accomplished poachers, so he was not surprised to find that the odor of the stew was very pleasing—rather more so than many of the stews that had bubbled away before the kitchen-fire at Valle Crucis.

The outlaws, pleased with their afternoon's work, passed stone jars of ale back and forth between them while their prisoners sat on the floor in a corner of the room. Simon and Master Shreve were virtually ignored for the best part of an hour, but the gentleman was in no mood for conversation. He heaped muttered curses upon the head of the outlaw chief and repeatedly threatened vengeance, but it was half bluster and half delirium, and Simon continually urged him to be quiet lest he arouse the wrath of their captors.

"Well," said the outlaw chief, when he finally turned his attention back to his prisoners. "Master Shreve has paid for his supper with good silver coin. How will you pay for yours, Brother Welshman?"

"I thought I had been brought here to read you the tale contained in the manuscript," Simon replied. "Is that not price enough?"

"It would be price enough for me," the chief admitted, "but I'm an educated man. To my lads it would seem rather more like penance, especially now they're merry with the ale. Can you do aught else that might please them more?"

"I can sing," said Simon, frankly.

The outlaws laughed at that, as if they did not believe him, but their chief put on a show of exaggerated delight.

"Then you must sing for your supper, in the grand old tradition," he said. "But I warn you—we want none of your accursed cantos, none of your troubadour French and none of your gibberish Welsh. The only thing that we'll accept in fee is a good English ballad. Can you give us that?"

Simon's repertoire of English ballads was not extensive, but there was never a man in the world, be he Churchman or Welshman, who did not know at least a few of the most popular songs of his day. He immediately began to sing a ballad about a shepherd boy lamenting the death of the girl who was to have been his bride. Although it was mournful, and had not a single hint of impropriety about it, the outlaws fell silent and listened respectfully to the end.

"Well, boy," said the outlaw chief, "you're uncommon honest for a Churchman. You can sing, and no mistake about it. You've earned your supper. If you'll give us another when we've eaten, we'll be in your debt, and we'll see you safely back to the road in the morning."

The stew tasted as good as its aroma had promised, and Simon sipped it gratefully from a wooden bowl, gladly fishing for fugitive pieces of meat with his fingers. The robber chief came to sit beside him on the floor, bringing his own bowl, and broke a loaf of bread, which was only slightly stale, offering a quarter of it to the monk.

"Now," said the outlaw. "Tell me what else is in this tale of yours—not the whole of it, but the gist."

Simon gave a brief account of the tale, explaining that it told how the Holy Grail had been given into the charge of a company of Welsh Benedictine monks who—fearing that it might fall into pagan hands in a time when the island was torn apart by the strife of war—had conveyed it secretly to Yorkshire, where they had hidden it away beneath an altar-stone in a little church in the village of Cockayne. He went on to explain how he had found the manuscript among those left to the Abbey by Prince Madoc, where it must have lain unread for more than a hundred years, and how the Abbot of Valle Crucis had written to Rievaulx to ask whether there actually was such a place as Cockayne.

The outlaw's brow furrowed when he heard that. "Is that why the Abbot of Rievaulx wants your script? Does he think it might be the key to buried treasure?"

"He is a man of God!" protested Simon. "If he thinks there is the slightest possibility that the grail still rests in

Cockayne, his one desire must be to restore it to the Church, that it might delight the hearts of good Christians. Only an outlaw could think of it as *buried treasure*."

Even as he spoke these words, however, Simon wondered if he might have been foolish in telling the tale to the outlaw. What if the brigand band rode north in the morning, directly to Cockayne? There was little doubt that they could get to the village long before he could arrive at Rievaulx. Suppose the grail *had* been buried at Cockayne, and was resting still where the monks had laid it? What a calamity it would be if the cup were to fall into the hands of such a man as this!

Simon realized, perhaps with a pang of conscience, that he had been thinking of the manuscript as a romance, like that of Chrétien de Troyes or Robert de Borron, and had given no thought at all to the possibility that it might be a true account. Now, as he watched the outlaw chief unwind the scroll again, he wondered whether he had been blind to the truth.

"The ink is poor," the outlaw said, staring at the script, "and the handwriting is poorer. Even the parchment is badly-made. This is not the work of a careful copyist working patiently in a monkish cell. When was it inscribed, do you think?"

"Not much more than a hundred years ago," Simon said, wishing that he were not so confident of the estimate. "During Madoc's lifetime, for sure."

"Then it's certainly a romance," said the outlaw. "It can be nothing else. And as soon as the Abbot of Rievaulx finds out that there's nothing buried beneath the altar-stone at Cockayne, it'll be cast aside and forgotten—gone forever. Good riddance to it."

"It will not be lost," Simon assured him, having been stung to annoyance by the outlaw's dismissiveness. "The fresh copy that I made at Valle Crucis will last a good deal longer than a hundred years, and will certainly be copied again if I have aught to do with it. What has been written down and committed to the care of the Church can never be lost—that is the whole virtue of writing."

"Nonsense," said the outlaw. "Writing relieves men from the responsibility of keeping what they know within their heads. What is copied and re-copied a hundred times might survive, but that which is not thought worth copying is bound to be utterly lost. I say again: as soon as it is proven that nothing is buried beneath the altar-stone at Cockayne, this silly tale will be condemned to oblivion. That ballad you sang will outlast this script by a thousand years, let alone a hundred, because there's reason in its sweetness for ordinary men to remember it, and preserve it in their heads."

Simon was by now half-convinced that the outlaw meant to establish for himself whether anything was buried in the church at Cockayne, and to do so before the Abbot of Rievaulx could mount an expedition on the Church's behalf. He reassured himself, however, that if the tale *were* true—which he could not quite believe, as it seemed so obviously a romance—then God would certainly prevent the outlaw from finding the grail. After all, if the adulterous knight the French misnamed Lancelot could only see the grail in visions, by virtue of his sinfulness, a Jewish thief would most certainly not be allowed to lay a finger on it, no matter how loudly he proclaimed that he was a man of honor.

That last thought reminded Simon of a question he had wanted to ask before—and he thought it wise, in any case, to change the subject.

"Why are you so loud in proclaiming your refusal to hurt anyone?" the monk asked the outlaw. "If they catch you, they'll hang you as a common thief, whether you've hurt anyone or not. You can't expect the slightest mercy from the law—especially given that you're a Jew."

The robber chief laughed at that. "Dolt," he said, not altogether unkindly. "It's not for the law's benefit that I take care to spread the news that I'm a gentle thief, who will not hurt anyone unless he has to—it's to reassure my future victims. If they know that they'll not be injured, they're far more likely to hand over their belongings meekly. If they feared for their lives, they'd be more disposed to put up a fight. There's always the odd fool like that man beside you, who'll fight regardless, but his servants had far more sense. They'd heard my name before, you see. In these parts, I'm as famous as any Frenchified knight who ever went hunting the Holy Grail."

Master Shreve, who had been sullenly listening to the conversation, reacted to this with his usual bullishness, pouring more curses upon the outlaw's head and swearing that he would have his revenge very soon.

"An outlaw is merely an outlaw," said Master Shreve, as he concluded his tirade, "no matter how many men have heard his name. Once hanged, you'll be forgotten in a day— and I'll see to it that you're hanged. Make no mistake about it."

"You're an uncommonly tedious dinner guest," the outlaw said, "and a silly one to boot. I might be remembered long after you're forgotten, and the Abbot of Rievaulx too, simply for having my name set into a ballad like the one my young friend sang before we settled down to eat. One ballad, if it has a good enough tune, will outlast a thousand tattered parchments like the one he's carrying to Rievaulx."

Master Shreve's sole response to this was a curse, but Brother Simon found himself rather intrigued by the possibility. He had always had a secret hankering to compose a ballad or two—while regretfully recognizing, of course, that any such activity was quite incompatible with his religious duties.

"I fear that you are wrong, sir," he said, teasingly. "There are plenty of ballads that tell of bold knights, and plenty which tell of lovesick shepherds, but there are no ballads about outlaw Jews. In order to be sung and sung again, a ballad must have the sympathy of its audience—just as a text, if it is to be copied and copied again, requires the sympathy of scribes."

"Then we must do with the ballad what scribes do with the substance of their texts, at the behest of their Norman overlords," the outlaw retorted. "If Welsh bully-boys, no better than outlaws themselves, can be disguised as French knights of unbearable piety, for the sake of making their stories palatable to the patient scriveners of Christian England, then a Jewish brigand might be disguised as a heroic Englishman fighting for a cause. Transform me, if you will, Brother Balladeer, into an Englishman through and through.

Give me worthy enemies to oppose—shift me back in time if you need to, for there's a certain respectability in antiquity. Change my name, if you like—but only a little, for we must not dabble in the purest fantasy. Reuben the Jew won't do, but there are Englishmen a-plenty named Robin, and my father's name was Hud, which will pass for English readily enough, although folk like Master Richard Shreve of Nottingham would have reckoned him a dirty foreigner. Only make a ballad of me, Brother Songbird, and repeat it in that glorious voice of thine, and I'll wager that my name will be on the lips of men far longer than that of any hired thug who ever laid false claim to knighthood."

"Perhaps I will," said Brother Simon. "Perhaps I will. In fact, I'll give you a solemn promise to do exactly that, if you'll give me your word in exchange that you'll not set foot in the church at Cockayne for at least a year and a day."

The robber chief laughed uproariously at that, and offered Simon his hand to clasp. "Gladly, lad," he said. "Gladly indeed—and you know full well that you can trust me, for Reuben the Jew is famed from York to Sherwood as the most honorable outlaw who ever stalked these roads."

* * * * * * *

In the morning, after a tolerable night's sleep beneath a solid roof, Brother Simon and Master Shreve were guided back to the Selby road, while the outlaws rode away to the east—conspicuously taking the direction opposite to that in which the cottage lay.

"We'll meet again, Sir Brigand, I promise you," the gentleman said—but he waited until there was only Brother Simon to hear him.

"It might be wiser to avoid that meeting," Simon advised him, "unless you want your body pierced by a dozen arrows. You left him with no reason to think charitably of you."

"Unlike you, I suppose?" Shreve retorted, hotly. "I never thought to hear a man of the cloth speak so softly and so cravenly to a thief and murderer. Everything they say about the Welsh is evidently true."

Brother Simon prudently made no reply to this insult, preserving a dignified silence while the two of them walked to Selby, where they found Master Shreve's servants— including the coachman—waiting dutifully at a very pleasant inn.

Brother Simon reached Rievaulx five days later, and was received with moderate hospitality, although he was required to sleep in an outhouse, without even a mattress of straw, because the Abbey was so crowded

The Abbot of Rievaulx did indeed send a deputation to Cockayne to dig beneath the altar-stone. His men found nothing. If the Holy Grail had ever been there, it was there no longer.

If Brother Simon ever made the ballad he had promised, he certainly would not have mentioned it to his confessor— and my tale must therefore leave the matter unresolved. But I am reckoned to be one of the best storytellers west of Neath, and I assume that the Church agrees with me, or your Abbot would not have granted you permission to write this down, and I can testify to this: I, at least, have never heard the name of Reuben the Jew, or Robin Hud, spoken or sung in any inn-yard in Wales. I think we may be perfectly confident that the name of an outlaw braggart cannot possibly be long remembered in a Christian land whose wisdom is in the charge of faithful clerics like yourself.

[Editor's note: having no competence of my own in the Welsh language, I must take it on trust that Dr. Evans has rendered an accurate translation of this remarkable document—or, at least, as accurate a translation as is compatible with the avoidance of too many inconvenient archaisms. Given that Dr. Evans holds a post at a good university and still attends chapel at least twice a year I think we can be confident of the story's substance, even if he has permitted himself the occasional embroidery in its dialogue. My own role has been restricted to the preparation of Dr. Evans' handiwork for the printer.

It is, of course, well-established that the earliest ballads featuring Robin Hood date from the late fourteenth century and that their setting does indeed seem to be South Yorkshire

rather than Sherwood Forest; the present manuscript, if it is to be reckoned anything more than a romance, may help to explain that confusion. It is, of course, extremely unlikely that any further evidence will ever turn up, and it is not at all surprising that the earlier manuscript to which this one refers has been utterly lost; Brother Simon's northward course to Rievaulx was followed only a year later by another traveler, whose devastating effects are noted en passant *by the storyteller: the Black Death.]*

LUCIFER'S COMET

Richard Halley's only son was born in 1986, the year that Halley's Comet made its much-anticipated seventh passage through the inner solar system. It seemed only natural that he should name his son Edmond, by way of acknowledgment, although he had not the slightest idea whether his own forefathers shred a common line of descent with the famous astronomer. It seemed only natural, too, that he should do everything he could to make his young son proud of the name that he bore.

As an infant, Edmond slept in a room whose walls and ceiling were lit by phosphorescent stars, arranged with great care to duplicate the form of the constellations: constellations that were then hardly ever visible through the polluted air of Greenwich. As a youth, Edmond received a series of telescopes and other astronomical aids for his birthdays, and was taken on family holidays to places where the air was clear and the stars shone in all their glory. As a young man he was given virtual reality links to the produce of every new space telescope launched into orbit. It often seemed that the only authentic conversations he ever had with his anxious and introverted father all began with the words: "Look up there, Edmond—do you see...?"

His mother called him Eddie, but to his father he was always Edmond.

In view of these formative experiences, it is not entirely surprising that Edmond's greatest dream and only ambition was to discover a new comet of unparalleled brilliance. The one named after his namesake was, of course, due to return again in 2062 but he knew that it would be a mere shadow of its former self. Indeed, when he took up the science of astronomy in earnest, he soon learned that its appearance at the time of his birth had been something of a disappointment to its patient anticipators. The world had hoped for a fine display, but it had been presented with an object hardly visible to the naked eye, of a luminosity so poor as to be almost negligible. That became the only fear shadowing his ambition: that he too might be a failure, not bright enough even to be evident to an untutored eye.

He was, at any rate, successful enough in his studies to be head-hunted to the USA and appointed to the team analyzing data from the first telescope erected on the far side of the moon: a perfect vantage-point from which to scan the sky for comets. He was also lucky enough to catch the tail end of a wave of fashionability that attributed some practical value to his mission; the brief upsurge of Millennial fever that had passed while he was still adolescent left in its wake a genuine anxiety about the possibility that the Earth might be struck at any time by an object big enough to wipe out half or three-quarters of all the species living on its surface.

Once he was a professional astronomer, of course, Edmond's surname began to seem more like a joke than a celebration. In order to differentiate himself from his predecessor he took to signing himself Edmond L. Halley, and if he were asked what the L stood for he would say "Lucifer". That was his own little joke, because Lucifer meant "light-bringer" and thus expressed—in a subtle and scrupulously unserious fashion—the hope that a comet might one day come his way that would put his namesake's shabby relic to shame.

* * * * * * *

After a few years, Edmond decided to be more assertive in making demands of fate, and he changed his signature to E. Lucifer Halley. When a few years more had passed—by which time his father had died of skin cancer—he dropped the family name altogether and became Edmond Lucifer, thus ensuring that if and when he did discover the comet that would make his name famous, it would be universally recognized as *his* comet, and not merely the second in a string founded by someone else.

"If that's what you want, Eddie," his mother said, when he told her of this decision. Her maiden name had been Rowbotham, and she had been very glad to have the opportunity to change it to something more fitting.

It wasn't necessary for Edmond to go to the moon in order to work with the Farside Reflector. The relay-system that brought the data back was complicated, but it had been very well-designed. He could slip on a VR hood anywhere in the world and see exactly what the Farside Reflector was seeing—or, rather, photographing—although there wasn't actually much point in doing that, because the team had a Cray to crunch all the numbers and turn the data into more manageable formats. For reasons of propriety, however, he chose to live as far away from the nearest city as he could possibly contrive. Even way out in the wilderness there was an unhealthy measure of atmospheric pollution blurring the scintillant halo of the Milky Way, but he liked the heat and the aridity of the desert and he soon educated himself to like the loneliness too. He lived as an astronomer ought to live, with the stars and planets for his dearest and most intimate companions.

The first half-dozen new comets that the Farside Reflector detected were mere minnows and Edmond declined the opportunity to have his name attached to any of them. His fellows made a joke of the fact that he was waiting for the big one, but he didn't mind—even a joke carried an implication of consent. He knew that he had to wait for the right comet, and he also knew that, when it came, he would be able to claim it. It would be his turn, his prerogative, his destiny.

According to the proverb, all things come to he who waits. Although proverbial wisdom is not entirely to be trusted, it proved its worth in this particular instance. When Edmond had waited long enough, the comet came. When he telephoned home to tell his mother the good news, she was delighted.

"That's marvelous, Eddie," she said. "Your father would have been so proud of you."

The Cray soon calculated that Lucifer's Comet was the biggest that had ever been named; it promised to be the brightest ever to appear in the sky while human observers had been around to marvel. It was a mere dot when the Far-side Reflector first registered its existence, and it was still a mere dot when Edmond Lucifer reported the discovery to the world, but the potential brightness of the object would probably have dented the world's indifference even without the Cray's careful computation of its orbit. As things turned out, though, the computation added considerably to the publicity that the comet attracted.

The Cray's calculations declared that Lucifer's Comet would cross the Earth's orbit less than twenty thousand miles away from the planet's position. From the moment this datum was first published, a few frightened individuals began to wonder publicly whether the computer might be wrong and—if so—by how much. Their fear was not taken seriously at first, but it proved infectious, and the wider it spread the greater its intensity grew.

Scientists and mathematicians immediately began to appear on current affairs programs broadcast by TV stations all over the world, assuring the public that the information gathered by the Farside Reflector was very accurate indeed, and that the calculations left hardly any margin for error. Expert after expert assured their constituencies that Lucifer's Comet would pass spectacularly but harmlessly by, and that everyone in the world would be free to enjoy the magnificent show it would put on.

Proudly and patiently, the world's astronomers explained to the public that Lucifer's Comet was a ball of mixed ices larger than any that had come tumbling towards the sun since human beings first turned curious eyes to the firmament of stars, and that those ices would sublimate in magnificent profusion to paint a beckoning finger across the face on Creation. Soon, they said, the comet would begin to grow a tail—and what a tail it would grow!

The astronomer who waxed most lyrical about this prospect was, of course, Edmond Lucifer, the bringer of light whose name the comet bore.

* * * * * * *

The fact that the scientists and mathematicians were absolutely certain that the comet would not hit the Earth didn't stop people worrying. Ordinary people had never trusted scientists and mathematicians—or, for that matter, science and mathematics—and diehard alarmists continued to raise disturbing questions.

What if the comet were deflected from its present course by the gravity of a planet or an asteroid?

What if the sublimation of its ices caused the comet to break up in an ungentle fashion, so that the fragments began to follow different and deadlier trajectories?

Called upon to answer these questions, Edmond Lucifer and his colleagues had to admit that such possibilities could not entirely be ruled out. Their tentative *caveats* about the slight possibility of their calculations being disturbed by some unexpected event was widely taken as a license to be terrified—and the name of the comet quickly began to took on a very different significance.

All over the Earth people began talking of the object— which was still invisible to the earthbound naked eye—as the Devil's Comet.

The discoverer of the comet discovered, to his chagrin, that in times of great stress—and the twenty-first century was, in many ways that had nothing whatsoever to do with astronomy, a time of almost unbearable stress—civilized people were just as inclined as their barbarous forbears had been to blame messengers for the quality of the news that they brought. Edmond had thought of himself as a bringer of wonderful news, but there were many who took leave to disagree with him outspokenly, and their numbers grew rapidly as the anxiety spread.

Alas, the name which Edmond had chosen to distinguish himself from his illustrious forbear was ready-made to become a focus of near-universal alarm. It began to be rumored that he had changed his name for the most sinister of reasons, and that he was indeed a secret disciple of Satan, perhaps the anti-Christ himself. Even among the scrupulously atheistic ranks of professional scientists, the name Lucifer began to be spoken with a condescending sneer or frank disapproval. The great majority of the experts who undertook to appear on TV to reassure the world that all was well, and that the Earth was perfectly safe, began to take great care to distance themselves from the man for whom the comet was named.

"He was not its real discoverer," these pundits hastened to say. "He was merely one member of a team, and it happened to be his turn to attach his name to the object—which he was allowed to do as a mere matter of courtesy. The vanity that prompted him to refuse to let the comet be known by his real surname, on the grounds that it had been attached to a comet before, is, of course, something ill-befitting a true scientist. The perversity that guided his choice of pseudonym is more ill-befitting still."

Edmond protested his innocence in vain; he was damned by the public and his fellow professionals alike.

"Don't listen to them, Eddie," his mother said, when he complained of the injustice. "They're just jealous. Mind you, you could have called it Rowbotham's comet, if you'd wanted to."

Edmond's colleagues on the Farside Reflector project expressed their solidarity at first, but they changed their minds when the anxious publicity grew more intense. They tried to change the comet's name, insisting that its "real" name was, and always had been, DR3-C41, but they were far too late. In the eyes of the world, the approaching object was Lucifer's Comet, and Lucifer's Comet—-or the Devil's Comet—it would remain.

The agency administering the Farside Reflector dismissed Edmond from his post—with not a whimper of protest from any of his former colleagues—but that made no difference to the public's perception of the project. Nor did it make a difference to the increasingly hateful popular perception of poor Edmond, who had to give up trying to justify or explain himself in the media because of the naked hostility generated by his every appearance in public.

* * * * * * *

By the time the comet was clearly visible in the night sky—to desert-dwellers if not to city folk—Edmond Lucifer's adopted name had become an object of dread.

One night, while sitting alone at the window of his desert home, Edmond realized that, in coming true, his great ambition had destroyed him—that his triumph was a mockery, and that his future was irredeemably bleak. The quiet light of the stars, which shone so brightly above him, was suddenly transformed in his disillusioned sight from a wonderful and loving radiance into a stern and malevolent glare.

He had no difficulty at all in picking out the faint dot that was Lucifer's Comet, nor in perceiving mockery and menace in its glitter.

"Curse you!" he screamed, although no one could hear him. "Damn you to Hell! I wish you *would* break up, and shower the Earth with a thousand deadly meteorites!"

The curse was, of course, utterly impotent. The Cray hooked up to the Farside Reflector dutifully calculated, in its patient fashion, that the comet had actually exploded at least thirty minutes before Edmond spoke these fateful words—but he took no comfort from the calculation, which he had to find in the pages of the press just like any other fearful follower of the world's implacable progress.

"Is the world going to end, Eddie?" his mother asked him, when she too had read the news.

"I don't know," he told her. "Nobody does. We'll just have to wait and see."

There were, of course, several weeks to be spent in waiting. Edmond had to go into hiding when a vengeful mob came to burn his desert home. Things became so bad that he daren't even phone his mother any more, lest the call be traced by dangerous eavesdroppers. By the time the shards of the comet arrived in the vicinity of the Earth he was by no means sorry to see its countless offspring.

For one fabulous night the sky was filled with shooting stars, which lit up the sky as if it were day—but when morning came, the dust of the multiple impacts blotted out the sun. The world was plunged into an awful darkness, which brought winter to the tropics and withered every crop in every field.

With its foundations ripped out, the precariously-balanced civilization of the twenty-first century crumbled into a terrible anarchy. The war of all against all demolished nation-states as easily as it turned cities into festering sores of violence and disease.

The last phone call Edmond Lucifer made to his mother was very brief. "It's not your fault, Eddie," she said. "Your father meant well, and I should have married Bobby Murgatroyd anyway."

"It wouldn't have made any difference," he assured her, insincerely. In fact, it *would* have made a difference—not to the world, which would have suffered the same fate regardless, but to *him*.

"We're all going to die, aren't we, Eddie?" his mother said, tearfully. It had been a long time since he had last heard her voice dissolve into sobs.

"Not all," he said. "A lot of us, but not all."

He was right. Within a matter of months the whole world had become a desert. Billions died in the course of the next few years, but the world of the twenty-first century had billions to spare.

In time, the dust settled again and the sky cleared, so that the sun might shine by day—and the stars by night.

Eddie Rowbotham, as he now called himself, never looked up at the stars again. He kept his eyes and his thoughts firmly fixed on the ground. He didn't feel any particular sense of loss; he just kept telling himself that it wasn't safe to go out after dark. He spent the rest of his life trying to make people like him, by trying to fit in, but it never worked. He just didn't have the gift.

* * * * * * *

In the new mythologies adopted by the newly-forged tribes whose members scraped a living from the ruins of the old world, the name of Lucifer was once again attached—by mistake—to a literal Devil. Within a few generations, though, the fearful figure had been reduced to a mere phantom, invoked as a petty curse and deployed in macabre jokes.

By the time the remainder of the comet came back to complete the process of destruction, the fateful syllables of Edmond Lucifer's adopted name had become utterly meaningless.

THE MIRACLE OF ZUNDERBURG

For thirty-three years, Helmut Arion, a tradesman in the northern town of Zunderburg in the region of the Neverlands, was known to his acquaintances—he had no friends during that time—as "the miser". Sometimes, when times were hard, those who were forced by circumstance to patronize his shop went so far as to call him "the sorcerer", because it was when times were hard that he made his greatest profits, depriving his customers of their money with such magical efficiency that they felt as if the blood were being leeched from their veins.

Helmut had long considered himself to be utterly innocent of all sorcerous skill, although he did admit that, in a demon-haunted world, it was difficult to be absolutely certain even of one's own virtue. He exercised his leech-like powers merely by outbidding all other buyers to purchase surplus grain in years when the harvest produced more than the people of Zunderburg needed to eat. Having stored the produce, he would sell it, for as great a profit as he could command, in years when the regional harvest was poor. When shortages were so acute as to cause famine, he would dole out his winter measures with the utmost care, often leaving his poorer clients bereft of all possessions and barely alive when the following summer eventually came.

"Who but the trusted minion of an evil spirit," his detractors were wont to say, "could keep half the town on the brink of starvation by the exercise of his meanness? Who but the demon-led could be so lacking in charity?"

On more than one occasion during the thirty-three years of his career as a corn-chandler, angry mobs stormed Helmut Arion's house and looted his warehouses, while crowds of onlookers cheered wildly, and called for him to be hung from his own shop-sign. The town constables and the mayor's men-at-arms always took care to save his life, however, and the greater part of his manifest property. The mayor and the constables resented his prices as much as anyone, but relied on him nevertheless to see their households through times when food was in short supply. Such episodes never put an end to Helmut's endeavors, because he kept hidden reserves in deep cellars protected by clever locks, where he also kept his gold-filled coffers. After each outbreak of mob violence, these reserves would be sold at even higher prices, and rationed even more frugally, so as to cover both his losses and his inconvenience.

Helmut's wife, Gertruda, was a full partner in his enterprise. She kept his accounts, and matched goods to be sold against leaden weights in a balance so uncommonly clever that it was universally believed to have been manufactured by demons. She handled his better clients with considerable charm, but was as impatient as he with beggars and wheedlers. Husband and wife loved one another with an avidity only a little less than that which they lavished upon their gold, and although they had no children they were reasonably happy.

Sometimes, malicious tongues alleged that it was, in fact, the ever-smiling but barren Gertruda who must be the servant of some seductive goddess, and that Helmut was merely a wretch who had pledged his soul to her in return for erotic favors and the benefit of her uncommonly clever balance. Their long-haired tortoiseshell cat was sometimes alleged by the same rumor-mongers to be a familiar spirit, but the she-cat was so plump and so easily intimidated, even by mice, that the charge was difficult to credit.

Helmut Arion and his wife offered no formal prayers or sacrifices to any of the Nine Gods which had officially-sanctioned shrines in Zunderburg. This gave further fuel to the rumors alleging that, while everyone else was offering dutiful prayers and legitimate sacrifices in the hope of a bountiful harvest, the Arions were casting spells to ensure that there would be hailstorms in May and droughts in July. Such talk remained submerged and impotent, however, until an exceptionally cold and miserable April brought a mendicant preacher to Zunderburg, singing the praises of a new god, of whom no one had ever heard before, whose name was Ynori.

* * * * * * *

Ynori's disciple was thinner and dirtier than any holy man that had ever been seen before in the northern reaches of the Neverlands, and commanded some attention on that score alone. He was content at first to speak to the people at road junctions and in the courtyards of inns, where the clamor and urgency of his voice won increasingly long pauses from many passers-by.

"The end of the world is nigh," he cried. "These are the last days, when the evil magic of sorcerers and witches runs riot throughout the world and the old, worn-out gods have lost the power to prevent it. There is no significant task before us now but to prepare for the judgment of Ynori, the youngest and last of the gods of the Neverlands. Signs and wonders prophesied by the initiates of Ynori have already made their appearance, and their import is clear. It is time for the good among you to turn to Ynori, who is the only god that can now protect you. If there is any among you who knows of sorcery and witchcraft, it is your duty to denounce its perpetrators, for your community must be purged before the end. Divest yourself of your worldly vanities! Woe to the rich and the greedy! Woe to the servants of demons! Repent your sins!"

Some senior citizens who heard these prophesies and adjurations remembered that they had heard their like before, cried on behalf of other gods, some forgotten and some still remembered among the Nine. Many younger folk were, however, inspired by them, for the winter had been excessively hard, and there were many people in Zunderburg who felt that they were almost as hungry and almost as wretched as the preacher seemed to be.

"The day of reckoning is coming!" these enthusiasts cried. "We who are on the brink of starvation shall be saved by Ynori, while the misers and witches who torment us will be damned by him. Judgment is at hand, and the petty sorcerers of Zunderburg must be purged, so that they might burn for all eternity in Ynori's secret Hell."

At first, the priests of the Nine Gods who were officially established in Zunderburg were openly contemptuous of the newcomer, but when they saw that a substantial fraction of the people had been captivated by his rantings, a few of them began to wonder if there might not be profit in his method. Soon enough, other gods began to side with Ynori in declaring that the end of the world was nigh, that it was time for their followers to repent their past follies and vanities and that the community must be purged of the demon-led.

Those priests who were initially inspired by their divine patrons to adopt a different course soon found that their congregations began to dwindle, and many were forced to seek further enlightenment—whose usual result was to add another voice to the doom-crying chorus. By the time that Ynori's apostle had been in Zunderburg for a fortnight, four of the Nine had been pledged to Ynori's support, and the neutrality of a further four was wavering. The only god whose priests remained steadfastly aloof from the apocalyptic fervor was Ikol, whose supporters called him the Eternal Nonconformist.

The first time that the itinerant preacher came to the street in which Helmut Arion's shop was situated, the corn-merchant ignored him, even though the preacher took sufficient heed of his audience to direct a certain amount of slanderous cant in the Arions' direction. Helmut Arion was not a man to be swayed by mere criticism; long endurance of the spite of his neighbors had inured him against common abuse, and the words of anyone ill-fed usually made no impact upon him whatsoever. Having measured the temper of the crowd once the preacher had concluded his business, however, he sighed in anticipation of worse to come.

Helmut knew that he ought to make the usual preparations for another outbreak of mob violence, which had been likely ever since the winter snows set in, but he found, on due reflection, that he had no appetite for another fight. At the ripe old age of fifty-five, and after thirty-three years of commerce, he felt that his strength and patience were too near to exhaustion.

* * * * * * *

On the night after the preacher's first visit to the street where the Arions kept his shop, while rumors of their sorcerous activities were being whispered in a hundred inns and attics, the anxious conversation of the husband and wife was interrupted by a discreet knocking at the door of heir house.

When Helmut opened the door to reveal a man who face was invisible within a capacious hood, his first instinct was to slam it shut again, but the visitor interposed his foot between the door and the jamb with such obvious dexterity that Helmut immediately leapt to the conclusion that he must be a very accomplished hawker.

"Whatever you're selling," Helmut said, brusquely, "We don't need it."

"But you do," the man with the intrusive foot replied.

Helmut did not recognize the voice, and was therefore surprised when the man drew back his hood just far enough to let his face be seen.

It was the preacher, the devout follower of the unknown god Ynori.

"If you have come to sell me salvation from your vile slanders," Helmut Arion said, ostentatiously refusing to open the door wide enough to allow the unwelcome caller access to his living room, "I repeat that I do not need it."

"I believe you do," said the preacher, "but I would never be so presumptuous as to offer something for sale that is entirely within Ynori's gift. All I have to sell is a meager miracle."

"Ah!" said Helmut Arion, who had reason enough to consider himself a man of the world. "You mean the kind of miracle that would prove my innocence of all charges of sorcery and commercial malpractice. You mean the kind of miracle that would bring about a marvelous conversion to pious faith, and deliver me into the good graces of your silly godling and his imbecile followers. You mean the kind of miracle that would make me hand over a tenth of my wealth in order to establish a shrine to that petty god in Zunderburg and purchase its official status."

"Actually," said the preacher, "I think I might obtain official status for such a shrine by means of another miracle, if what my converts tell me about the mayor's bad habits has a drop of truth in it. Alas, that does not empower me to offer you a discount—and the tenth that you mention was last year's price, before cruel winter set in. Now that the end of the world is so obviously nigh, mere material wealth has been so comprehensively devalued that the cost of even a modest miracle has doubled."

"I do not need it," Helmut Arion repeated, frostily. "Do your worst—I have not long to live in any case, and no children to protect."

"Oh, I know how brave you are," said the preacher, his practiced voice hoarse with menace, "but I do not believe that you have nothing to lose. Even a man who has nothing but death before him has reason to prefer a good death to a bad one, and you have a partner in witchcraft that you love very dearly, if rumor can be trusted. On the other hand, the fact that you are so old and childless should assist you to see the wisdom of not clinging to your earthly possessions as hard as you have been wont to do in the past. No one can judge the temper of a town better than I, and I can assure you that the coming season will be exceedingly hard for sorcerers and their kin. It will not need a miracle to keep the constables and the mayor's men-at-arms at home, when the people of Zunderburg decide that the corn you have hoarded is theirs by right, and does not need to be weighed out according to the uncommonly clever balance that your witch-wife keeps. Believe me, Helmut Arion—I never saw a man in such need of a miracle as you."

"Perhaps you are right," Helmut Arion admitted, after a slight pause for consideration. "Perhaps I do need a miracle."

He drew back the door as if to let the hawker of salvation in—but when the self-satisfied preacher removed his foot, reaching out a hand instead by which he hoped to support himself on the jamb as he passed through, Helmut slammed he door with all his might.

The catch could not snap shut because the preacher's thumb was in the way, but the force of the collision broke the bone and made the preacher howl in agony.

When Helmut Arion drew the door back again to release the trapped digit, the preacher was still too preoccupied with pain and distress to be able to pronounce the threats and curses that swelled in his lungs. It was Helmut who spoke, saying: "If a miracle is required, I believe I shall supply it myself. I have never been a man to buy cheap and shoddy goods when the best is available at little more expense."

While the cursing preacher shambled away into the night, clutching his broken thumb to the voluminous folds of his cloak, Helmut returned to Gertruda. "I fear, my dear, that the end of the world really is nigh, this time," he told her. "We are too old for this kind of foolishness. If there is nothing significant for any man or woman to do but prepare for judgment, then we must prepare as best we can."

"What do you mean?" she asked.

"I mean that the time is ripe for a miracle," he said. "The only thing to be settled is the name of the god to whose credit is should be accounted. A week ago we might have been spoiled for choice, but circumstance and cowardice have reduced the field to two. I have never been one for worship, but if a clever tradesman needs a god to intercede on his behalf, he surely ought to select the least dishonest."

"Ikol," said Gertruda, without hesitation.

"Ikol," Helmut agreed.

* * * * * * *

On the following morning, the mendicant preacher paid a visit to Helmut Arion's shop, leading a troop of fifty loyal followers. He did not go in, being content to stand outside where his clamorous and urgent voice would be more clearly heard.

"Ynori came to me in a dream last night," he cried, the timbre of his voice suggesting that he was still in considerable pain. "He told me that of all the sorcerers in Zunderburg, of whom there are many, the very worst are Helmut Arion and his witch-wife. Of all the demon-led, they are the most malevolent—and this is proved by the fact that, even as I slept, communing with Ynori, they contrived to break my thumb in the hope of obscuring the divine word. Woe to the demon-led! Woe to the miserly! Woe to the exploiters of the poor and hungry! Prepare to meet thy doom, Helmut Arion, for damnation is at hand!"

The preacher would undoubtedly have continued in this vein until the crowd had swelled to twice its number, and even its laggards had built up a serviceable fever, but Helmut Arion came out of his shop at this point and announced that he too had had a dream, in which he had been visited by Ikol and instructed to prepare for judgment. As a result of what the god had told him, he said, his shop would be closing down in three days time, and in order to dispossess himself of his stores he would have to lower his prices considerably.

"While stocks last," the former miser declared, "A penny of anyone's money will buy what was yesterday three pennyworth to a baker, four pennyworth to a miller and five to those who mill and cook their own loaves."

The preacher opened his mouth to continue his own tirade, but he was bundled out of the way by the rush to follow Helmut Arion back into his shop—and, although the disciple of Ynori continued to harangue the queue that extended half the length of the street, he could not make them feverish. They were too busy discussing, wonderingly but earnestly, the miracle that Ikol had wrought: the miracle that would put bread on their tables.

By mid-afternoon, the queue outside the Arions' shop was a hundred strong; when it closed that evening two hundred were still outside, fully a hundred of whom remained where they were, determined to keep their places until morning. When Helmut and Gertruda returned to the shop the next day, a thousand people were jostling one another in the street, fighting with fists, knives and ploughshares for the privilege of gaining access to the premises. By mid-day, five had died and more than a hundred had been cut or bruised.

By this time, all Helmut's ready supplies were gone, but deliveries continued to arrive at irregular intervals as his various cellars were emptied. The queue did not diminish in the least, but, as more and more people secured their supplies, tempers were calmed, and everyone praised generous Ikol for the miracle that had made the miser repent his former wicked ways.

On the third day, when the last supplies of corn were brought out of his storage-cellars, Helmut Arion gave half of each load to the constables and the mayor's men-at-arms, in return for promises that they would protect him against any residual resentments that might be harbored by the adherents of Ynori. These promises were gladly given, but by the time the stocks were exhausted, the town was nearly united in proclaiming that Ikol had always been the best and most generous of the Nine Gods of Zunderburg, and that his protection was all that anyone required to see them safely through the world's end and into the paradisal afterlife.

Having closed his shop, Helmut Arion said to his wife: "Our coffers are overfull of gold, even at the prices I have been charging. Should we give some of it to the poor, do you think?"

"Certainly," said Gertruda. "A tenth would be quite adequate, I think—and the priests of Ikol can surely be entrusted with the responsibility of doling it out. Let us keep back enough to buy a sizeable cottage in a pretty part of the countryside, a good field, a well-built barn, a modest flock of healthy hens and a small herd of milking cows. Then we and our servants can leave the town with our consciences clean, and await the end of the world in quiet humility."

This was exactly what the former miser did. He bought a very pleasant two-storey cottage backed by a sturdy and capacious barn, near a run-down hamlet where accommodation for his servants and laborers would be easily and cheaply obtainable. He bought the best flock of laying hens in the district and half a dozen cows, and gladly retired from the hurly-burly of commerce and town life.

The tortoiseshell cat hated her new surroundings at first, but soon learned to stand up to the mice which infested the barn. Like her owners she lost a little of her plumpness, but eventually began to take pleasure in providing for her own sustenance.

* * * * * * *

News soon began to filter back from the town, which assured the Arions that they had made a wise decision. After a period of rejoicing, when even the poor dined richly on good quality bread, old routines and recently-imported fears had reasserted their conflicting authority. Even though the disciple of Ynori had decided that his message might be more profitably spread elsewhere, Zunderburg seemed to have been hit by a veritable epidemic of witchcraft, which was turning the good fortune dispensed by the great god Ikol and his convert Helmut Arion into a plague of ill-luck. Accusations of all kinds were being bandied back and forth, and the priests of the eight gods that had realigned themselves with the followers of Ynori had become even more zealous than their model.

The spring that followed the vile winter was just as poor, with May and June being disturbed by torrents of rain and hailstorms, all of which were blamed in Zunderburg on witchcraft. Dozens of suspected sorcerers were hanged or beaten to death. When summer finally began, the sun burned fiercely for weeks on end, and those cornstalks which had survived the floods and the battering hail shriveled in the heat. In Zunderburg this too was blamed on witchcraft, and dozens more suspected sorcerers had their throats cut and their houses burned—but all to no avail.

Meanwhile, although Helmut and Gertruda's lettuces and turnips thrived, and their hens laid prodigiously and their cow gave abundant milk, the local grain harvest was the poorest of the decade. The farmers who were the Arions' new neighbors told them how fortunate they were to have repented in time, and to have won the full favor of Ikol's generosity—generosity that the god, perhaps understandably, seemed disinclined to extend to followers who were unwilling or unable to offer such abundant testaments of faith.

As things went from bad to worse in the Neverlands, times became difficult even for Helmut Arion and his wife, but they loved one another as well as they ever had, and they were wise enough to be content with that part of their fortune which they had kept. They were thinner when September came than they had been since the day they married, but they knew well enough that they had escaped much worse by virtue of the timely miracle that had saved them from the wrath of Ynori. The knowledge that they were in harmony with Ikol, by virtue of their renunciation of a fraction of their wealth, was a great comfort to them. Possessing no more material wealth than was necessary, they believed that they had everything and more, by virtue of their new-found spiritual wealth—and there was no doubt at all that their old acquaintances were in a substantially poorer way.

In Zunderburg, the people survived in spite of the poor weather and the ceaseless responsibility of witch-finding. Thanks to Ikol's miracle, they had dined more abundantly during April and May than they had previously been wont to do, even in autumns that had followed bountiful harvests. Helmut Arion's price-cutting had forced lesser merchants to cut their own prices, at least for a while, with the result that their own reserves had been all but exhausted before the end of May. The gold that Helmut Arion had given away, even after the priests had taken their commission, had given the poor sufficient purchasing power to buy all the vegetables that came on to the market in the spring, and plenty of meat besides. Throughout the summer, the butchers had found it easier to dispose of their wares than they ever had before, and more animals had been sent to the slaughterhouse than usual. Unfortunately, the depleted herds and flocks were incapable of increase during a summer when much of the produce that would have gone to feed them was diverted to the town.

When November came, the prices asked for grain, meat and cabbages soared to unprecedented levels—but the poor had been well-fed, thanks to the generosity of Helmut Arion, and they knew that they were better equipped to endure a period of hardship and hunger than they had ever been before. When December arrived, though—with unprecedented ferocity—many of the people were still repeating the words of the itinerant preacher, who had long since returned to the south, but had let a sturdy legacy behind. "Eight of the Nine Gods agree that the end of the world will be upon us very soon," the townsfolk whispered in inns and attics alike. "The day of judgment cannot be long postponed, when we shall reap our just reward for all the effort we have expended in purging our community of sorcerers! The hard winter is proof positive of that."

But the cold persisted through January and February, and the world endured.

In March, hundreds of people went to the door of Helmut Arion's shop, where they had always been accustomed to go in desperate times, but the building was derelict. No hidden supplies of corn were secreted in its cellars; no gold was in the former miser's coffers. Nor was there anyone else in the town who had been able to maintain stores of corn through the remarkable events of the previous year.

* * * * * * *

As the cold and damp extended their unceasing clutch even into the cozy depths of their comfortable cottage, Helmut's faithful Gertruda fell ill. She had been as healthy as anyone in the region, but she was as old as he. Although she suffered no considerable pain, the life began ebb out of her. The end of March brought her to the point of death, but she told her husband that she did not mind.

"It is as you said," she told him. "The end of the world was, indeed, only a little while away. Mercifully, we made our own arrangements to meet it, and produced our own miracle according to our own thrifty habit. We have nothing to fear."

Gertruda's woebegone husband tended her while he could, but he went to fetch a priest of Ikol when there was nothing else to be done. The priest blessed the dying woman, assuring her husband that she was undoubtedly bound for paradise, because there was no one in the world who stood higher in the favor of Ikol than she.

"Zunderburg stands in sore need of another miracle now," the priest added, by way of an aside, "Although the snow is melting, times are very hard. The search for sorcerers has been renewed, for it seems that the followers of the Eight Gods did not clear them out at all, although they were sure that they had. There is more evil magic worked within the town nowadays than anyone had ever thought possible—but we followers of Ikol are armored against its effects."

No sooner had the spirit fled Gertruda's body than the weeping Helmut sank to his knees, proclaiming his desire to follow her into the infinite. He prayed that Ikol, who had already vouchsafed him one small miracle for the sake of his salvation, might vouchsafe him another now—and when he laid his head upon his wife's pillow, the life flowed out of him like blood from a wound.

The priest of Ikol returned to the town, proclaiming that Helmut Arion had died happy and fulfilled, having done everything in life of which he was capable, and having been received into the arms of Ikol as the most precious of all the Eternal Nonconformist's servants. The priest advised the townsfolk that there was a valuable lesson to be learned from all that Helmut Arion had done in response to the miracle which had warned him of the impending end.

Unfortunately, the increasingly desperate witch-hunters who owed allegiance to the remaining Eight Gods paid little heed to the priest of Ikol, and refused to take any lesson from the heart-warming parable of the miser's repentance.

Although thousands of the townsfolk came to the brink of starvation and hundreds toppled over—each and every one of them direly cold, sickeningly hungry, horribly miserable and bitterly regretful—the world itself went stubbornly on, and the lamentations of the living became gradually more clamorous.

"Where, oh where, is the promised Day of Judgment?" was a cry which went up from many a bedside, echoed in every attic and every inn. "Why have we not been delivered from the malice of sorcerers and the demon-led?"

There was, alas, not one among the inhabitants of Zunderburg who had yet begun to suspect or understand that the day in question was already behind them, and that their own powers of judgment had already been weighed—against the mass of their frightened, stupid souls—in an uncommonly clever but scrupulously honest balance. Such is the invariable way of things, in the Neverlands.

THE CULT OF SELENE

Professor Amarinth became fascinated by the Cult of Selene simply because so little was known about it. He was not the kind of historian who reveled in abundant documentation; he had always been drawn to the mysterious and esoteric, to those phenomena which hovered in the margins of the *recorded*.

Even the ancients, it seemed, had been in a hurry to forget the cult. In common with so many abandoned faiths, the little that was known about it had to be reconstructed—with all due skepticism—from the writings of its enemies, who regarded it as a dangerous heresy. The task of reclaiming the truth from a ragbag of slanders is never easy and its results are always uncertain, but that was the kind of task that Amarinth loved.

It was easy enough to determine that the daughter of Helios and Eos had been the earliest of all the Greek moon-goddesses, but that she had eventually been replaced as an object of reverence by Artemis and Hecate. Only two myths concerning Selene had survived to be written down, and even those had sometimes been transferred to the credit of one or other of her successors. One was the rumor that Pan had once seduced her with the gift of a beautiful fleece, whose metaphorical significance was no longer evident. The other—the more substantial, and hence the more intriguing of the two—was the tale of the handsome youth Endymion, who had redeemed the single wish she had promised him by choosing to sleep forever without aging a day.

All that was known about the rituals followed by the initiates of Selene's cult, when Amarinth began his work, was that they were organized around the phases of the moon—an item of information so obvious that it hardly qualified as knowledge at all. It was unanimously affirmed by the cult's detractors, however, that the followers of Selene had adjusted all their ideas and habits of life to the changes that overtook the moon's face as she waxed and waned, with an extremism judged by these unsympathetic commentators to be near to madness. Amarinth soon became convinced that this was the key to the cult's essence, and also to its disappearance.

Amarinth came to believe that the followers of Selene must have indulged in wild excess when she was full and lapsed into quietude when she was new, and that this had applied to mental activity as well as physical activity. Reading between the lines of the few remaining references convinced him that this alternation of attitude had cut far more deeply than mere ritual observation. When the moon was full, the followers of Selene must have been calculated orgiasts, feeding all their appetites as gluttonously as they could; when the moon was new, they must have been the sternest of ascetics.

In itself, this would have posed no particular threat to the prevailing social order; the rites of Dionysus, which had offered the same periodic license, had lasted much longer. Amarinth hypothesized that it was, in fact, the philosophical alternations indulged by Selene's disciples that had caused the greater affront. When the moon was full, the Selenists were prepared to indulge any wild fantasy of the imagination, becoming more fanciful than any lyricist—but when it was new they became the most rigorous of skeptics, more cynical than the Stoics. As the tenor of Greek philosophy had become devoted to the ideal of *consistency*, the indefatigable Amarinth concluded, such gyrations of conviction must have come to seem uniquely obscene, their alternation appearing to be worse than any kind of unintentional mental instability, however unreasonable or unedifying.

Amarinth realized that the Selenic cultists must have artificially induced in themselves the psychological syndrome that is nowadays labeled "bipolar disorder", and developed that condition to a pitch of awkward perfection. He understood that their attunement to the phases of the Moon must have been more intimate and more fundamental than the scholars who had gone before him had guessed or presumed. Far from being an unimportant eccentricity, which had failed the test of endurance, the conduct of the Selenists had embodied an alternative paradigm of "mental health": a radically different notion of how human life ought to be lived and how human thought and sensation ought to be organized.

Amarinth realized, too, that the "sleep" which had claimed Endymion—and, he presumed, all the most devoted of the goddess's male followers—must, in fact, have been an altered state of consciousness. At first he thought that it might have been a depression so deep as to constitute a living death, from which no recovery was possible, but he came eventually to the view that this made nonsense of the careful mysticism of the myth. He deduced that the sleep of Endymion must instead have been an ecstatic state, in which thought became so infinitely elastic as to constitute an escape from the prison of "reality", from which time itself had been effectively banished.

Once he had reached this conclusion Amarinth saw that the apparently unconnected tale of Pan and the fleece was a blurred counterpart of the tale of Endymion, likewise allegorizing the experience of those who moved beyond the pendular swing of spiritual rigidity and manic frenzy. They must have entered a fluid state, which seemed to doubtful observers to be akin to the "panic" which the oldest god of all was reputed to visit upon mortals he wished to tease and confuse.

Amarinth was content at first to pretend that his investigations of the cult of Selene were purely academic, but he eventually saw through his self-deception. Now that the God of the scriptures has been exposed as a hollow sham we are all in search of worthier deities, whether we admit it or not—and Amarinth was honest enough to recognize, in the end, that he had been drawn to the study of the Cult of Selene by the deep-seated cultural necessity of its revival.

Amarinth concluded that the current medical practice of stabilizing manic depressives by feeding them lithium carbonate, however appropriate it might seem in the more troublesome cases, was exactly the reverse of what more enlightened individuals might and ought to require. He set out to find a compound which would have the opposite effect, exaggerating the effects of the syndrome to the point at which the cycle might dissolve into the "sleep of Endymion": the waking dream in which all ideas became equal, all actions possible, all destinies irrelevant.

He sought, in brief, to open a transcendent doorway to long-forgotten realms of human experience.

In order to test the compounds he investigated, Amarinth had, of course, to recruit a number of acolytes to the re-emergent cult. This proved easy enough; the contemporary intellectual climate, dominated as it was by the idea of postmodernism, was highly conducive to such seduction. Participation in the rites that he designed proved highly addictive to most of the neophytes he welcomed into the fold, and he was delighted with the alacrity with which they learned to savor the extreme contrasts of the full and new moons. Others called them lunatics, of course, but they wore the name with pride.

Because he had been in his post for many years, Professor Amarinth was still subject to the contractual privileges of full tenure, and he was able to disregard surly complaints from his colleagues that he had overstepped the bounds of legitimate research in the field of history. It took ten years of sustained labor and constant experimental testing before Amarinth produced his first Endymion, but, once his medicines had been properly formularized and sufficiently refined, he had no difficulty in repeating his triumph.

That first Endymion is still dreaming his glorious dream, among a steadily-growing company of eternally youthful "sleepers". These children, born of the magical union of Selene and Pan, are a constant delight, not only to their High Priest, but to everyone they encounter. They have such vivacity and zest for life, and even though they are reckoned mad by common people, they are happier by far than ordinary mortals. They do age, of course, in purely vulgar terms—some have suggested that they age even faster than the norm, because too large a fraction of their resources of energy are devoted to the production of the gorgeous golden hair that covers each and every one of them like a fleece— but no one who has seen them dance by the glorious light of the moon could regret their exultation or their marvelous versatility.

This, then, is the gospel according to Amarinth, the prophet of Selene:

> *The old gods are returning; a new spirit is setting them free from the bondage they have too long endured.*
>
> *The steadfast sun is in eclipse and the changeful moon is on the rise.*
>
> *Chaos is come again to overturn the imperium of consistency; belief and conviction are free to run the gamut of conceivable attitudes.*
>
> *Let us rejoice and rest, let us sing and sleep, let us dance and dream, for there is indeed a time to every purpose under Heaven.*
>
> *Above all else, let us be free of the deadening hand of the average; away with the mean and exalt the meaning.*
>
> *We were not destined to be dull, but to be glorious; only hear the music of Selene, and we shall be glorious again.*

His detractors say that he is mad, and that his cult will wither and perish as its predecessor did, but that is only to be expected.

ICE AND FIRE

I went to see Jake in the hospital last week—a matter of duty, blood being thicker than whatever, and all the other crap I come out with when people ask me why. He has a TV in his cell, so I knew he'd have seen the documentary about the Elephant Man, but I hadn't read the papers attentively enough to know about the other thing.

"It wasn't neurofibromatosis," he told me, as if it were a point he'd been trying to prove for years. "The poor sod had Proteus Syndrome. *Proteus Syndrome!*" Jake is a confirmed hypochondriac. He'd been suffering from imaginary neurofibromatosis for years, but it looked as if he'd just got a second opinion.

"I know," I said. "Trouble is, they didn't actually explain what Proteus Syndrome actually *is*, did they? It's just a name—a fudge-word. Laudanum puts you to sleep because of its soporific effect; the Elephant Man's flesh went haywire because he had Proteus Syndrome. It doesn't add anything."

"It's what I've been saying for years," he told me, looking right down his nose at me the way he always did—and not just because I was his little brother. He looked at everyone the same way, except for Mum. Mum wouldn't stand for it.

"You've never said a word about the Elephant Man," I pointed out, taking refuge in pedantry the way I always had. Mum had stood for that, and Jake had never been able to stand her standing for it. "You never even heard of Proteus Syndrome till Tuesday night."

"Molecular memory," he retorted. That was one thing he had said, over and over and over. He was a big fan of mo-

72

lecular memory. He loved the idea of anonymous plastic blobs that retained their original shape when they were heated. He loved talking about the way the DNA in an egg-cell somehow "remembered" whether the egg was supposed to grow into an ostrich, a whale or a human being. He loved telling people that the dinosaurs hadn't become extinct at all—that it was just a matter of their molecular memory being dispersed in the flesh and blood of others creatures, us included. "Nothing ever dies" was another of his catch-phrases. "Things just get misplaced for a while." I dare say that all the devils in Hell are as expert in quoting scripture.

"Sure," I said, in my best sarcastic tone. "We're all Elephant Men really. It's just that our DNA has forgotten the trick of bringing out the full potential of our ugliness. It's too dilute in the blood, just like the secret of making dinosaurs."

"Merrick was a good man," Jake insisted. "A good man betrayed by his turbulent flesh. It could happen to anyone or everyone, any day. You know what's in the ice, of course?"

"What ice?" I asked.

"Trouble with you," he said, "is that you have shit for brains. Always did have. Just a *pretty face* and a *lying disposition*. Louis Frank's ice. Louis Frank of the University of Iowa, who said that a NASA satellite had recorded chunks of extraterrestrial ice entering the Earth's atmosphere way back in 1986—only none of his shit-for-brains colleagues would believe him until now. They've got the pictures now. Happens all the time, it now turns out. Constant bombardment. They still think it's just ice of course, except maybe Fred Hoyle and Chandra What's-his-name? You know, though, don't you? You know what's in the ice, because I told you, didn't I?"

"More molecular memory," I said, tiredly. "Evolution from space. Packages of DNA like pieces of a jigsaw, avid to get into the bloodstream, looking for the right-shaped holes."

"Damn right," he said. "Anyone and everyone, flesh and blood and plastic bone. You got the right-shaped hole, Mister Shit-for-Brains, you could be the next Elephant Man. We all could. Tomorrow, or the day after, we could all get the Proteus Syndrome. We could all start becoming what we always were, except that we forgot. Any body any time any fucking way at all. It's in the papers—all you have to do is read. It's on TV—all you have to do is look."

"Not everybody sees things the way you do, Jake," I told him.

"Damn right," He retorted, as if it had been intended as a compliment. "Blind bastards with shit for brains can't see their hands in front of their noses, or the blue blood inside their veins, every hemoglobin molecule longing to fill the oxygen-shaped hole and turn to good honest red. People don't have a fucking clue what's inside them, what they *are*."

"If you keep on like this," I told him, "they're never going to let you out. You know that, don't you?"

Of course he knew it. He knew everything. The only way you can hurt someone who knows everything is to remind them of the things they'd rather not know. If you're a big brother, though, you can't ever admit that a little brother has the power to hurt you. That's not the way things are supposed to work on life's little battleground.

"I could get out," he told me. "Don't kid yourself that I can't get out. There's guys in here have killed six, seven times. Kids, mostly. They don't like to let *them* out, especially now we're in the Computer Age. Registers, see—they get out, people notice, spread the word. I'm not so rare. More people kill their mothers than a mother's boy like you could ever imagine. Murder's just memory, see. Molecular memory. It's in the ice, like everything else. You know what'll happen when the ice caps melt in ten, twenty years time? Then we'll see some serious Proteus Syndrome, some real Promethean Heat. Ice and fire, Danny boy, ice and fire. That's all we are and all we'll ever be. Can't do a thing about it, except pray that we keep on forgetting everything we ever forgot, keep on dispersing everything we ever dispersed."

Jake's scrupulous self-education hasn't been confined to science; he reads the classics too. Tragedies only, of course. Promethean heat is from *Othello*, when Othello realizes what it is he's done. Promethean heat is what would be needed to bring Desdemona back to life, if only she could be. Jake believes in Promethean heat, of course, because in his world nothing ever dies; it just gets temporarily mislaid—like Mum and the dinosaurs.

"The doctor says that you have to face up to what you did," I told him, a nice as only nice can be when trying to be nasty. "The doctor says you have to admit it to yourself instead of always trying to worm your way around it. Worming your way around it proves that you're still fucked up, a danger to society. It gets you nowhere."

"Tell that to Ouroboros," he said, and laughed like a drain. I always hated hearing him laugh, even when I was a tot. You might think that tots can't hate, but they can, and they do. It's in their blood. They hate—but they can't act on their hate. It's different for big brothers. The time comes when they're bigger even than their mothers, and still remembering all the times when they weren't. Mum would never stand for Jake's nonsense, even when he got to be more than big enough—but she laid herself down and out for it all right, when she had to, and never got up again. Ice and fire, you see: either the one melts or the other fizzles out. They use to say that Jake and I were chalk and cheese, but they were wrong. We're ice and fire, just like Jake and Mum were ice and fire. Now Jake pretends that it's the whole world's tragedy—and maybe the universe's too—but it isn't really. It's ours. It isn't even in the blood, although he'd like it to be. It's just something he did, and nobody else.

"You're not the Elephant Man, Jake," I told him. "You're not some kind of science fiction mutant. You're not the next phase in human evolution, forced by circumstance to grow up as a feral child, all warped and misunderstood. You're just a fuck-head who killed his mother, and if you can't accept that you're never going to get out of here."

"You wish, Danny boy," he said. "The pipes, the pipes are calling, Mister Shit for Brains."

Sometimes, I wonder what I do wish. I think, on balance, that I want to have my cake and eat it too. I do want my brother to face up to what he did, and admit everything that's there to be admitted, but I don't want him to be let out because of it. I want him locked up forever—but I'll always go to see him, the obligations of blood being what they are. I'll always share a little bit of his imprisonment, a little bit of his insanity, because I just can't get away from it. I would if I could, but I can't.

"The day is coming," he told me. "All the signs are there. We think we're so fucking great because it's nine thousand years since the last really big one hit. We think the ice has let us alone forever, that the fire is safely contained within the mantle of the Earth—but it's not. We think we're *it*, but we're not. We're just a part of it, a set of pieces with hollowed-out souls, waiting for the next ice-rider to come along and make us all into monsters. It's happening, Danny boy. It's happening. The day is coming. Any day now, the ice will free the fire. Any day at all."

"The people at Heaven's Gate had the right idea, then," I said. "Time to go to a better place, in the belly of the mother-ship."

"There *is* no better place," he assured me. "You may think you're in a better place already, because you aren't *here*, but you're wrong. We're all here—we just don't know it yet. I could get out. There are people here who never will, but I could get out if I wanted to. I'd rather be able to see. I'd rather be able to see the truth and tell the truth. It was all your fucking fault, you know. If you hadn't come along, with your pretty face, she'd never have forgotten me. If you want people to face up to things, you should start with yourself."

Perhaps he's right. Perhaps, if I hadn't come along, she'd have stood for it all, because it would have been all that she had. I can face up to that, if I have to. I can face up to Jake, no matter how big he is and how ugly. I can look at myself in a mirror, and see exactly how right he is and exactly how wrong—but I don't have anything to be ashamed of. Mum and I were just fine; we fit together perfectly.

"You still don't see it, do you?" Jake said. "Even though they got pictures. The ice is always falling. Always."

"Sure, Jake," I said, as cruelly as I could. "It falls on the just and the unjust alike—but it doesn't turn us all into raving maniacs. For that, you have to have the right kind of hole. Yours is in the head." I could have added *right in the middle of your ugly face* but I didn't. I'm supposed to be helping him, after my fashion. The doctors think of me as an ally, a therapeutic aid.

As I said, perhaps he's right. Perhaps, if some huge hunk of ice hadn't hit the earth sixty-odd million years ago, the dinosaurs would still be around instead of their molecular memory being dispersed in the bloodstreams of a million other species. I hope to God they never come back—but sometimes, when I'm alone in an empty room, I just can't help wondering whether Jake might be right in spite of everything. Maybe nothing does die, at least not forever. Maybe all that we can ever hope for is to be temporarily mislaid.

Like Jake says, the Elephant Man was *good*. He didn't deserve Proteus Syndrome—but nobody does, not even Jake. That isn't enough to drive it to extinction, though. Deserving doesn't come into it at all. Ice freezes and fire burns, because that's the way the world is. I wish it weren't but it is. I suppose the dinosaurs would feel the same way, if they were capable of feeling anything at all.

I miss Mum—but I don't miss Jake. I go to see him, regular as clockwork, come rain or come shine, but I don't do it because I love him, or because I think it might help to make him better. Truth to tell, I don't want him to get better. I want him just the way he is—not because I couldn't hate him just as well if he wasn't, but because it's the way he is. He's ice and I'm fire, or maybe the other way around. He's crazy and I'm not. He's ugly and I'm not. He's a killer and I'm not. I don't know what we'd be if you added us together, but I think we're a hell of a lot better dispersed. Some things are—but I don't necessarily count the dinosaurs among that number. Some people can't understand why I keep on going to see him, just to listen to all that crazy talk about the end of the world being foretold in his flesh and in his tragedy. I tell them it's just a matter of duty, blood being thicker than whatever...but sometimes, when I'm alone, especially in an empty room, I just can't shake that feeling that he *might* be right. Any day, any way, the world could just end, in ice or in fire, without really ending at all.

Things being what they are, I don't suppose I'll ever be completely free of feelings of that sort.

SELF-SACRIFICE

There is a ritual element to matters of this kind, which must be carefully observed. It is important that you make the correct selection, most particularly on this occasion, and the search—however uncomfortable it may be—must not be hurried.

It does no good to drive slowly along the usual streets, scanning the dim-lit ranks of careerist whores; authentic professionals are no use at all, however fresh and lean and tender they may appear to be. Girls of the right kind are never to be found on the usual pitches. The regulars will not tolerate them, not because they consider them to be competition (although they may be had cut price) but because they worry about the reputation of their streets, and do not wish them to become known as places where addicts ply their trade. In the civilized heartland of whoredom there is no worse strategy than to take one's stand in an area that is moving down-market; the honest tradeswomen who take a pride in being service sector professionals, who believe and hope that they are clean and wish to advertise their cleanliness—honestly or not—must at all costs steer clear of the dead-enders who are past caring about what they pick up or what they pass on, or anything at all except the magic powder that sets them free.

To find what you need, you must go where the derelicts go, into the Underworld beyond and beneath the enterprise culture, and there you must search with infinite care for your Eurydice. You must go deeper, into the innermost circles of Hell, in search of the derelict and the desperate, to find a girl who is not merely child-like but so exclusively dependent on her regular fix that she has utterly abandoned all self-regard.

There is no functional necessity in this, of course—she will undoubtedly be positive, as you are, and that may be taken for granted—but, in matters of this kind, aesthetic priorities are paramount, and it is aesthetic necessity which governs your choice.

You are duty bound to celebrate each anniversary as though it were the last—as indeed it might be.

When you do find her, she will be initially reluctant to go with you; that is inevitable. She is in Hell, but she is with the devils she knows, and you are a devil she does not. It is not that she fears what you might do to her; if she fits your requirements she will not be afraid of any kind of imaginable physical abuse, or being killed. What she fears is losing her connection. Her worst nightmare is that she might find herself in a place she does not know, where she does not know how to score. What she wants to do is to get into the front seat of your car and suck you off as fast as she possibly can, so that she can run with her wrinkled ten pound note to some pit of shadow where the Candy Demon always waits, ever-ready to do business. When you tell her that you want something very different, she is certain to hesitate. Even if you showed her five notes instead of one she would hesitate. So you show her something else: something white.

It wouldn't have to be genuine, if all you needed was to draw her into the car. If the quantity were right, the mere possibility would be promise enough; even here, hope has power enough to conquer cynicism. But in ritual matters of this kind, authenticity is of paramount importance. When you show her the heroin, it must be real.

Everything must be real.

Ideally, the girl should be intelligent. She would listen to you anyway, and her attentiveness will be mere performance in either case—it would be far too much to hope that she might care—but if she is intelligent, she will more fully understand what you say, and that is good. It does not matter what her reaction is—she will probably think you are mad, even if she does not say so aloud—but in this day and age, almost everyone holds the opinion that almost everyone else is mad; that is always the last defiant claim of an imagination which can no longer cope with the enormity and ugliness of the world.

After all, there is a strong case to support the claim that everyone is mad, or at least deluded. We think that we're in charge of ourselves and our lives, but we aren't. Those few who try to do their best for their loved ones, and for mankind, never do what needs to be done, and never even permit themselves to recognize what needs to be done. We can't control our fundamental urges and impulses well enough to render them harmless. If the world is moving, at last, in the direction of sanity, it is no thanks to Everyman; he is simply a fool and a madman, fiddling while the Human Empire burns. Nor, in spite of everything you have done, may you count yourself a shining exception. You can't avoid your share of the guilt, your share of the sin, your share of the madness. You must remember that, today of all days. You're no better than anyone else.

Once she has been lured into the back seat of the car, she immediately becomes a prisoner of the child-proof locks. It doesn't matter whether she is aware of it or not. She is, in any case, a prisoner of evil circumstance. The plush seats of the BMW have merely brought a poignant hint of luxury into the cold rigor of her meager existence.

You study her carefully in the rear-view mirror. Such are the boundless benefits of modern-day technology and the scientific perspective. Orpheus did not know what was happening behind him, and could not resist he temptation to look around as soon as he thought—wrongly—that it was safe to do so. You have a better understanding of the limits of possibility than he had, and your journeys into Hell always achieve their purpose.

This time, she is blonde, although it is not easy to tell because her hair is so dirty and hangs so raggedly about her face. The face is obviously good, though: thin and gaunt, with watery, haunted eyes. She wears an anorak and blue jeans, which hide her figure, but she is evidently half-starved. She has become accustomed to feeding her spirit rather than her body, and evidently knows well enough how superstitious conventional ideas about a healthy diet really are.

She is only five feet tall, possible four-eleven. It is hard to tell how old she really is—perhaps as much as eighteen, or even twenty—but she looks fifteen. She will certainly pass for a child when she strips down, if only by virtue of her emaciation. Authenticity matters in this instance, as in all others, but on this particular point, authenticity is compromised by ambivalent circumstance. This is Sally's twenty-first birthday, and the ninth anniversary of her death. Her image in memory is both twelve and twenty-one, at one and the same time; she is child and woman both, just as she is dead and also—by virtue of her reflection in the rear-view mirror—still alive.

When you stop in the underground car park and let her out she looks warily around.

"Here?" she asks, wearily, as though it makes no difference at all to her.

"Upstairs," you say. "The thirteenth floor."

She follows you to the lift—after all, you have the plastic bag full of powder in your briefcase: the bread of Heaven, the staff that supports her precarious life. You have become, in her eyes, the Candy Demon, the deliverer of sweet oblivion. You are her Grim Reaper, her Father Time, bearing a cup instead of a scythe.

If only she knew what a Reaper you are! But she will know, later, when the time comes for the most sacred part of the ritual. Then, she will hear your confession, and know what you are. She will not grant you absolution, and probably will not believe a word that you say, but she will hear the truth.

There is no gratitude in her eyes as she looks around the flat, no sense of wonder at all. If there is any speculation in her gaze it is a pathetic attempt to guess whether anything easily portable would be worth the effort of stealing it, should the opportunity arise. Alas for her ambitions, there is a marked dearth of ornamentation, and nothing to be seen that is made of gold or silver. Your tastes and inclinations have become increasingly Spartan since you became a widower.

When you lead her into the bathroom she is resigned but faintly resentful; she has no notion of ritual cleansing, but she must know that her face will be fairer, and her hair silkier, and her body more pleasant to the touch, once the stain of the streets has been removed. Perhaps that is what she resents: the obligation to provide sensual pleasure. She ought to be grateful for the chance to take a bath, but she shows no sign of it as you run the water. She should be alert to the possibility that your purposes might coincide in some respect with her own desires, but her attention is so narrowly focused on the magic powder that it has no scope for any other satisfaction.

She does not undress until you instruct her to do so, but she makes no complaint. She is not unduly ashamed or uncomfortable to be seen naked, nor to be soaped and scrubbed by your gentle hands. When you give her the clothes that you have set aside for her to wear she puts them on indifferently. She is not the kind of whore who plays parts like this as a matter of course, but she has heard her share of stories about the crazier kind of client and she is incapable of surprise. Perhaps she believes that she is acting out some stereotyped and vulgar cliché.

"I really need the stuff," she says, when it dawns on her that this may take some time, but she does not expect to obtain her reward so easily. You open the bathroom cabinet and show her the hypodermic, still in its sterile wrapping, and the rest of the apparatus, all ready for her. She has already seen the drug itself. For the first time some fugitive relic of her former curiosity urges her to say: "You a user?"

You shake your head. "It's all for you," you tell her. "You can take it all."

That makes her anxious; she has gauged the quantity and its value, and reckons this too generous a promise. She knows that she is not worth a tenth as much, on the open market, and wonders if she has been taken for a ride.

"Where'd you get it?" she asks, suspiciously.

"I'm a doctor," you tell her. "It's easy for me. I can get hold of any quantity without having to account for it. I cut it myself. It's perfectly safe."

Her fears are not altogether quieted. It is in her mind that she might, after all, have been brought here to suffer some hideous ill-treatment, perhaps cruel enough to break down the sturdy wall of her indifference to harm, but she knows that it is too late to pay attention to such possibilities. She allows herself to shepherded back into the sitting-room, squirming as she tries to make herself comfortable in the party dress that was made for a little girl.

Then you bring out the birthday cake, and light the candle, and display yourself for the harmless eccentric that you really are.

There are twenty-one candles: twelve white, nine black. You hesitate before explaining, hoping that she might be clever enough to deduce what is happening, to provide the beginning of the story herself. Perhaps she is—might that be a flicker of comprehension in her weak, red-rimmed eye?—but if she is, she will not voice her conclusions.

"My daughter," you say, as tenderly as you can, "would have been twenty-one today, if she had not died. I always have a party."

She nods. She thinks she understands. She knows how small and thin she is, and what kind of clothes she has been given to put on—although she does not know as yet precisely what she might be asked to do, if anything, when she takes them off again.

"Your name," you say, "is Sally."

She has sufficient sense of occasion not to contradict you. In fact, she reveals a certain flair for the dramatic by asking: "What did I die of?"

She is probably thinking of something like leukemia. It is tragically romantic when children die of leukemia. She is probably hoping that the answer is tragically romantic, because that will reassure her about the nature of the pantomime in which she has been invited to play a leading part.

"You were murdered," you say, staring at her face to catch her reaction. Because she has relaxed her guard a little, she does react, but the shock is subdued; her emotions are still anaesthetized, although she certainly needs her fix.

"You were knocked off your bicycle by a drunken driver," you explain. "You fractured your skull, broke your pelvis and ruptured your spleen, in addition to various minor injuries. It was a Sunday afternoon. The driver was a childless housewife aged thirty-nine, who had nothing better to do with her time than commit the occasional desultory adultery and drink herself stupid. She was banned from driving for four years but the judge thought that a custodial sentence would be inappropriate, presumably because she was middle class."

"Oh," she says.

"It was your birthday," you add, bleakly. "You died on your birthday."

"Oh," she says, again.

"It destroyed your mother. She wouldn't have caved in so soon, if it hadn't been for that. She'd have been stronger."

This time, she doesn't even bother to say "oh".

You sit down beside her. You have to blow out the candles yourself, before you cut the cake. You offer her a neatly-cut slice whose size is judged to perfection, and she looks down at it suspiciously. It is a sponge cake, dyed in pastel shades, with thick, soft, white icing and glutinous synthetic cream.

"You don't have eat it if you don't want to," you say, amicably. "I didn't bring you all the way up here just to eat cake. In a little while I'm going to fuck you, and then I'll give you the stuff. But it won't hurt to eat. Please."

This confirmation of the game plan helps her to relax. Perhaps she sighs with relief, thinking that it all makes more sense now, and that the ritual is crazy in an altogether commonplace sort of way. She thinks about saying: "Did you used to fuck your daughter?" but she doesn't. She isn't as impudent as some of her predecessors, although her thoughts run along the same lines.

"No," you say, as though she had asked. "I didn't ever fuck you while you were alive. I wanted to, very much, but I never did. I thought that it would constitute child abuse, and might cause you to have psychological problems in later life. If I could have been confident that you would continue to love me, I might have taken the risk, but I wasn't. Incest and child molestation get such a bad press, you see, and I wasn't able to assess the accuracy of the common opinion that girls fucked by their fathers always hate the experience. I didn't want you to hate me, so I never took my opportunities while you were alive. Now that you're dead, it's much easier. I

84

don't have to feel guilty about the fucking—only about the fact that it gives me a reason, however small, to be grateful that you were killed. If you were still alive, I probably never would have fucked you, unless you had gone out of your way to seduce me. I'm sure that happens, sometimes, but it may be just wistful thinking."

If she notices the play on words she doesn't react.

"Aren't you having any?" she asks, before taking the first bite out of her slice of cake.

You shake your head. "I never do," you say. "It's for you."

She is still suspicious, but she eats the slice of cake. She disposes of it rapidly, but not avidly; it is not greed which moves her but a desire to get on with things. Her attention is fixed on the moment when she will be given the superabundant supply of heroin, with which she gratefully will hammer one more figurative nail into her coffin.

The sugar in the icing and the cream conceals the bitter taste of the muscle relaxant. The dose is precisely calculated, as it invariably is, thanks to your long experience and profound respect for ritual. It will gradually rob her of the power of movement, but it will do no real damage, and she will remain fully conscious. It is necessary that she lies still, not in order that you might fuck her—she would, of course, lie still for that anyway—but in order that she will not become restive afterwards, when she must listen to what you have to say. She will be impatient for her overdue fix, but a vital part of the price will still remain to be paid, and it is necessary that everything should run smoothly.

"I loved you, Sally," you tell her, while the drug takes effect. "I loved you with a devotion and a passion that you probably cannot imagine. The sexual component of that love was only a tiny part of it—a belated extension of something much vaster and more profound. I loved you even before you were born, when you were merely an unformed idea. I am elderly, as you can see; I had long planned to have a child, in spite of the terrible state of the world, but I felt—deeply and sincerely—that I was not entitled to do so unless and until I had first accomplished something that would make the world a better place. I took my duties as a father seriously, you see.

I still do. Everything I did in those distant days I did for love: for love of the wife I had and the daughter I intended to have, for love of all the wives and daughters which good men and true would have. I could never care as much for my fellow men; I could not help but feel that they were the ones who had made Hell on Earth, while women and girls were merely their victims. I have always loved women—the *idea* of womanhood."

She opens her mouth to reply. It is bound to be something sarcastic; a person like her is incapable of understanding what you have just said, and incapable of sympathizing with it even if she did. Persons of her kind have no sentimentality left in them—but that is not her fault. She too was a child once: an authentic child. It is the world that has made her into what she is, obliterating all the potential beauty with which her mind and heart once overflowed. She is, after all, the victim on whose behalf you have labored all your life. She is the reason, the daughter, the idea.

She finds it unexpectedly difficult to speak. She hasn't yet lost her voice entirely, but she can't quite formulate the mocking words she intended to use.

You stand, and pick her up. She weighs very little; you have no difficulty in lifting her and cradling her in your arms. Just for an instant, anxiety makes her cling to you, as if you were indeed her father, come at last to rescue her from sore distress, come to repair her anguish with the protective embrace of your arms. But she cannot sustain the effort, physically or spiritually.

You take her into the bedroom and you lay her out on the bed. You undress her, one precious garment at a time, lovingly and reverently. Then you undress yourself, looking down at her all the while.

She is not entirely devoid of a sense of duty. When she realizes that you mean to fuck her without any protection, her eyes widen slightly, and the ghost of a frown creases her forehead. If she were able to mobilize her paralyzed vocal cords she would warn you. In spite of what she thinks you are, she would warn you. She does not wish you dead.

"It doesn't matter," you say, soothingly, while stroking her pale cheek. "I'm positive. I've been positive for years. We belong, you and I, to the same legion of the damned."

And then, for a while, you say no more. Actions speak louder than words.

* * * * * * *

The purpose of ritual is to dignify a mere event and thus transform it into something more significant, something more meaningful. The purpose of ritual is to magnify thought and action, to elevate them to a higher plane, where the particular may become general and one lonely act of love may symbolize the love that all mankind has—or ought to have—for the world which gave them birth and gives them sustenance. Through ritual, the tawdry becomes noble, the ordinary becomes extraordinary, and the mundane becomes supernatural.

Because this intercourse is a ritual, mere appearance becomes irrelevant. This is not a drug-addicted whore at all; it is your daughter. It is the idea of your daughter, the ideal of your daughter, the idol of your daughter. What you are doing is no mere obscene performance, and what you will achieve is no mere release of libidinous frustration. This is the perfect act of love, the ultimate celebration, made glorious by its very impossibility.

The flesh that you touch is her flesh. It has her texture, her odor, her vivacity. The rapture which you feel is the rapture of communion with her.

This is no illusion, no pretence; this is real.

This is, in fact, the only reality; all else is false. The entire world in which you live and labor, save only for this, is but a delusion laid before your eyes by a mad and spiteful demon. You are in Hell, even here and even now, but for this one extended, infinite moment in time you have the ecstatic power to transform that Hell, to redeem the world from its desolation.

You delay the culmination of the process and the inevitable decay of ecstasy as long as possible, but you cannot delay it for long. The experience is too powerful; it is too great a gift to have your daughter released, if only for a few precious moments, from the world beyond the grave. You close your eyes, hoping against hope that if you obey the cunning injunction of the Prince of Hell you might keep what has been covenanted to you, but in the end it is impossible.

You, as a scientist, must respect that. The impossible remains, and always will remain, beyond your reach.

* * * * * * *

Afterwards, you make your confession. While she is still present and conscious—though lost and probably frightened, in the strange, lumpen, useless body which you have helped her to borrow for a little while—you tell her what you were never able to tell her while she was alive. You explain to her why you did what you did, for her and for the world.

"Long before you were born, Sally," you say, patiently, "it had become obvious to the enlightened few that the world was in deadly danger—that the Great Mother of us All was sick, and that her children had become her unwitting enemies. There were those who said that it was the machinery which had run out of control, that it was all to do with automation and the polluting excrement of factories, but men of my kind—the doctors, the biologists—knew that was false. We knew that men did not require heavy machinery to poison rivers and make deserts, that subsistence farmers cutting wood for cooking fires could devastate ecosystems as efficiently as the makers of motorways and diggers for oil. We knew that the real, underlying problem was simply a matter of numbers. We knew that the sole solution, however unpalatable it might be, was to reduce the size of the human population. We also knew, though, that the only people who would voluntarily accept the necessity of having fewer children, or none at all, were people like us, and that we were too few to make any material difference.

"You must understand, my darling, that this was a matter of inevitability. Those of us who understood were a tiny minority—perhaps one in every million—but there was no doubt about what we saw. The world was descending into ecocatastrophe, like a huge lorry careering down a steep slope, unstoppably. People were complacent, because the effects they saw around them seemed to be no more than a series of minor nuisances, but that is what a man thinks when a mosquito bites him, unaware that the parasite is now in his blood, and that the havoc it will wreak, destroying his health and strength, is inevitable. The great majority of men have always been blind to the future, Sally. Even among those who can see, the majority feel themselves to be helpless, incapable of any constructive action save complaint.

"Only a few of us truly understood, and only a few within the few were prepared to act. Only a tiny, infinitely precious few, were prepared to take responsibility, to take upon themselves the burden of mankind's sins of omission and commission, to swallow the bitter pill of necessity. We had the means, in our laboratories; we had the will, because we loved the world, and loved our daughters; we had the courage, because we saw and understood that if we did not act, Mother Earth herself was lost.

"What was needed, my love, was a single vital move in the great game of life, which could save the world. We knew that no such salvation could be achieved overnight, or even in our lifetime, but we also knew that great oaks from little acorns grow, and that if only we could plant the right seed we might set in motion a train of events every bit as unstoppable as the juggernaut of world population. We had known for centuries what the three significant checks of population were: war, famine and plague. We were not the kind of men who could start wars, and famine was by then too blunt and powerless an instrument, but we were the kind of men who could engineer plagues. We were doctors, men who understood the elementary chemistry of genetics and disease. We had the knowledge and the technology required to devise and manufacture a new plague, and we had the intelligence to calculate exactly what kind of plague would do the job required of it.

"Our plague had to be the kind of disease that was immune to ordinary chemical defenses; it had to be a virus rather than a bacterium. It had to be the kind of disease which would kill all but a tiny fraction of those who contracted it, but not quickly; the cleverest parasite is the one that does not destroy its hosts but carefully preserves its capacity to spread. It had, therefore, to be the kind of disease which could lie dormant for a long time, spreading through the population insidiously. It had to be the kind of disease that could evade the body's own natural defenses, so that people would not easily acquire immunity to it, with or without the aid of inoculations to stimulate antibody production. We knew that, however deadly our plague might be, there would be some who would not die, because some would eventually reach a biochemical accommodation with the virus, but we knew that we had to ensure that only the strongest and the best were likely to survive to become the parents of a better, wiser, less prolific race.

"A group of a dozen men designed and created exactly such a disease. We worked in secret, under no one's orders. No government was involved in what we did; we and we alone were responsible for what we did. We knew exactly what we were doing, and why. We did it for entirely selfless reasons—for the sake of our children and our children's children. We decided in advance that none of us should profit from what we had done, or try to evade its consequences. As soon as we were certain that we had engineered a virus that met all our specifications, we inoculated ourselves with it. We moved quickly to create other, far more efficient, centers of infection, but we did not shirk our own responsibilities. We could only justify inflicting what we had made upon our fellow men if we were willing to sacrifice ourselves, and that is what we did. We destroyed all the evidence of what we had done, including ourselves. We accepted destruction, to prove that what we had done we had done for the benefit of others and the salvation of our Mother, the Earth.

"All the members of that tiny regiment of unsung heroes are dead, save for me. I am the last. There is a reason for this, although I cannot deny that pure chance has played a large part in ensuring my survival. Once a person has been infected by the virus we invented, you see, it lies dormant for some time—perhaps two years, perhaps ten, and in rare cases indefinitely. All victims of the virus become participants in a great lottery, waiting for their turn to sicken and die, but the lottery is biased. People who are weak with hunger, or very young or very old, or who suffer from some other disease or genetic deficiency, are more vulnerable than those in the prime of life and the pink of condition. Psychological factors play a part too: those who are under stress, or chronically depressed, or emotionally unstable, are more vulnerable than those whose lives are on a even keel, who are calm of mind and buoyed up by a sense of purpose, and are not eaten away by guilt or remorse or bitterness.

"It was not obvious to me in the beginning that I would be the last survivor of the initial group, but I have proved to myself that I am a stronger man than I ever thought possible. When you died, I might have followed you into the grave, but I did not. I fought back against the vicious whim of fate. I reminded myself that I am a solver of problems, a man of achievement, a man who had take it upon himself to save the world by obliterating the human surplus and preserving only the essential, only the best. I knew that I could undo the fact of your death, and its effect on me, if only I had the strength and the skill—and I did. I have brought you back from the Land of the Dead from the deepest pit of Hell to its outskirts, its earthly borderlands. Year after year, I bring you back— and as long as you can return, I may stay.

"I was never able to tell you this while you were alive— I was never able to confess what I had done to anyone, because I had sworn a solemn oath. But the oath cannot apply to conversations with the dead, and so I have the opportunity to explain what I have done, to ease my conscience, to justify my decision. I wish with all my heart that you were not dead, my darling—I would far rather that you had taken your chance among the ranks of the living, perhaps to become the mother of a daughter yourself—but I cannot change places with you. This is the only way in which you can continue to live, and in order that you may have this, I too must continue to live. I will continue, as long as I can.

"I will see you next year, my darling girl."

* * * * * * *

When it's all over, you let her use the bathroom to shoot up. She is entitled to her reward and her privacy. She does not know that she was drugged; she believes that her sudden incapacity was mere exhaustion, a weakness of her own, simply one more arbitrary manifestation of the inexorable deterioration of her body and her mind. She is even grateful for it, because it made the fucking less burdensome for her, and postponed the clawing agony of her dependence.

She shows no sign of remembering anything that you said, although she was conscious throughout. Her memory has discarded it as though it were a dream. That is understandable, and appropriate; it wasn't, after all, this shabby, skinny prostitute to whom you were speaking.

As you finally show her to the door she looks down, hesitantly, at the plastic bag full of white powder that she is trying to conceal about her person. There is such an abundance of magic there, such a cornucopia of promises.

She looks up at you, not afraid now that she is high to take a risk. Her caution is thrown to the winds on which she soars.

"I could stay," she said. "As long as you like. I'd be your daughter. I'd be anything and everything you wanted. You said you could get the stuff—that it was easy."

"It wouldn't work," you say, softly and paternally, as you open the door to let her out. "It couldn't work. You see, you're dead."

She curls her lip, abruptly transforming her impression from innocent, pleading temptation to malevolent, contemptuous wrath, and says: "You and me both, motherfucker."

And she is right: positively, inevitably, decisively right. But thanks to you, the world will one day be saved.

TO THE BAD

I think I ought to write the story of how my sister Cecilie went to the bad. Some of you will probably think that I have gone to the bad too, simply for wanting to write it, but that is one of the reasons why it ought to be written.

* * * * * * *

No one in the family had the least suspicion, while we were growing up, that Cecilie would one day go to the bad. When we were children, I was always the naughty one; Cecilie was always good. After a while, that kind of contrast came to be expected of us. Our mothers would shake their heads and fondly lament that it was always the same with a litter of two unless the two were identical twins. They were always looking out for us to disagree and be different, and because Cecilie was always so anxious to please, I was inevitably cast as the rebel. It wasn't all my fault.

Not that I could see this at the time, you understand; at the time, I thought it all came naturally to me: the breakages, the sins of omission—even—oh horror of horrors!—the lies and the *indiscretions*. It's only hindsight that allows me to see that it was all a kind of game. I was unwittingly nudged into being a living illustration of all the things that kids of our kind shouldn't do and shouldn't be, so that I could be patiently redeemed and straightened out. My childhood was made into a lesson, from which Cecilie and I were both supposed to learn what we need to know in order to get by.

It would have been a neat trick if it had worked, but it didn't.

The trouble was that this approach to our sentimental education made me question things, and there were some questions that never did get answered during the straightening-out process. I came to understand well enough about sins of omission, and lies, and the overwhelming necessity to *be discreet*, but there were other things about which the doubts remained.

One of them, as you will have guessed, was writing.

I first set down to write a story when I was eleven years old. It was a science fiction story about men on Mars—Yuri Gagarin had just orbited the Earth for the first time and I was hung up on the idea of space and conquering the universe. At first, the adults assumed that I was just doing my homework, but when I told Mother Thalia what I was really doing she asked Father John—my actual father—to have a quiet word with me.

"It's just not our way, Francis," he told me, gravely. "Writing is one of *their* things. It's necessary for you to go through the motions at school—that's all part of *fitting in*—but it's not something you can bring home. It's not something we ever do on our own account. Writing, you see, is a kind of indiscretion in itself. It *preserves* things, and there's too much danger of revealing something, even when you don't mean to. Our arts are the performing kind, which leave no material traces: music, singing, dancing. Cecilie is a lovely singer—you could have learned to play an instrument, if you'd only put your mind to it. You still could."

"It's a science fiction story," I assured him, earnestly. "It's not about *us*—it doesn't matter a bit whether the people in it are our kind or theirs; they just have adventures."

"That's a dangerous way to think, Francis," he told me, soberly. "It always matters whether people are our kind or theirs. *Always*. Forgetting that is the greatest of all indiscretions."

I abandoned my story, and decided that I would be a real astronaut instead of a science fiction writer. I must have nursed that ambition for a year or more before I finally became reckless enough to mention it to Mother Heloise. It was Father Valentine who was delegated to explain why it was just as bad as wanting to be a writer.

"You're old enough now to think about this sort of thing *realistically*," said Father Valentine sternly. He was the oldest of the co-husbands, and he always seemed scrupulously stern. "The world is becoming hazardous for people with secrets to keep, and we have to be very, very careful in selecting appropriate niches for ourselves. It's best to avoid anything that involves being closely scrutinized. Can you imagine what an astronaut must go through in terms of medical examination and testing? We can alter our appearance inside as well as out, but we couldn't be certain of passing for human under that kind of scrutiny."

I saw the sense in it. I understood what he was telling me. Even then, though, I began to see corollaries of his argument that disturbed me.

Father Valentine was oblivious to those corollaries, but Father Valentine had been born in 1830, and to him—as to the great majority of our kind—bureaucracy and medicine were just new-fangled nuisances that threatened our best-kept secrets. He couldn't see that doing our utmost to avoid all the kinds of scrutiny to which the humans had begun to subject themselves was a strategy that could only work for a little while longer, and which served to cut us off from certain benefits which the humans obtained from their new skills. He couldn't see that we ought to have our own legion of doctors, studying and refining an up-to-date kind of medicine for *our* kind. He couldn't see that, in telling our children to stay well away from any contact with X-ray machines or blood tests or operating theatres, for fear of being *indiscreet*, we risked cutting ourselves off from something very valuable.

Cecilie dutifully took not the slightest notice of the science lessons we had at school. She was a good girl, easily clever enough to appear conventionally dull. I was the rebel, too clever for my own good, who couldn't help being interested. It didn't help matters that I always seemed "young for my age" to my faster-maturing classmates; if there's one thing the average bully hates more than a smartarse it's a precocious smartarse. I assume that the bullies had a good laugh when the family pulled me out of school at sixteen, as soon as they could get us out of the system.

THE GARDENS OF TANTALUS, BY BRIAN STABLEFORD

* * * * * * *

In spite of the differences between us, Cecilie and I were very close. We were bound to be, I suppose, given that we were the only kids in an eight-adult household. Mother Lucrezia had had a three-boy litter fifteen years earlier, but by the time Cecilie and I were able to take notice they seemed to us to be uncles rather than brothers, and they soon passed on into the network.

When our turn came to be passed on—to begin our "real education", as Father Raphael put it—there was some talk of splitting us up, but we protested and all four mothers came in on our side. I think their most telling argument was that Cecilie would be a "stabilizing influence" on poor unreliable Francis.

Oddly enough, nobody took the trouble to explain to us exactly why we had to pass on. I presume that the mere fact that it was customary was considered explanation enough; our great respect for tradition is, after all, one of the things that are supposed to make us superior to those wild-hearted humans.

I remember thinking that I was very clever when I worked out the logic of it. It was like a flash of illumination when I first saw that those who are perpetually in hiding must always have hiding places in reserve; they must always have somewhere else to go when discovery threatens, and it must be somewhere that they know, somewhere into whose background they can fade. It isn't enough for one of us to be part of a single household; our links to other groups, even other families, must be many and complex. So, for thirty or forty years—three or four times as long as we spend in *their* schools, learning the geography and mechanics of *their* social world—we visit our kin, learning the geography and mechanics of our hidden and parallel world.

Ours was a small-town household in the north of England, so it was virtually inevitable that we should be passed on to kin in the capital city. Mother Lucrezia's litter had been passed on along the same route, thirteen years earlier, but things had changed since then.

London in 1967 was not quite the same place that London in 1955 had been.

* * * * * * *

Our aunts and uncles in the wicked city weren't nearly as protective as our mothers and fathers had been; we were there to learn, after all, and they had no intention of wrapping us up in cotton wool. We went out a great deal, together and separately. We made a great many connections, with the other kind as well as our own. It wasn't just Cecilie and myself who absorbed something of the human *zeitgeist*—there were other youngsters of our own kind around, who were just as fascinated by the fashions and the music and the ideas of the day.

In the beginning, I was the one who was curious and excited about everything that we did and everything we discovered. I was the one hungry to find out what was *going on*. Cecilie was nervous and intimidated, and took time to come out of her shell. As the months went by, though, the situation changed dramatically—and Cecilie changed far more than I did.

However interested I was in all the things that were happening, I always remained an observer: an outsider. I never lost the consciousness of being apart from it all. I didn't think of my apartness simply in terms of belonging to a different species; I was certainly no human-hater. I guess it was simply an attitude of mind. I still fancied myself as a pioneer of sorts, as an *explorer* of the vivid and confusing wilderness of sex'n'drugs'n'rock-and-roll (you have to say it like that, because it was all one thing, to those who were a part of it). Cecilie was different. Cecilie, once she had learned to love the life, loved it with all her heart. Once she had loosened up, she threw all her energies into whatever was happening. She went to the bad.

She went native.

It wasn't obvious to her, or even to the aunts and uncles we were lodged with, that what she was doing was going native. Father Valentine would have seen it immediately, but Father Valentine had come to seem to us—and even to our adult hosts, although at least one of them was old enough to remember Queen Victoria's Golden Jubilee—to be a boring provincial stick-in-the-mud. You see, we didn't think of the things that were going on as a purely *human* thing; in many ways, they seemed more *our* sort of thing: the music, the dancing, all the performances and displays and trips (which blew our minds in exactly the same way that they blew human minds, and made all our physiological differences seem trivial....)

Cecilie was far better prepared to take her place in that kind of culture than I was. I was a doubter and an explorer; she was more adept at fitting in—and she had such a lovely voice. It was a time and place extremely and fatally hospitable to talented singers, especially if they could be beautiful.

That's one of the corollaries of our talent for fitting in, of course; we can make ourselves dull, but we can also make ourselves beautiful, if we want to be. It must have seemed entirely natural to Cecilie that in adapting herself to an age of beautiful people she must make herself beautiful.

In fact, it was a sad mistake.

* * * * * * *

The aunts and uncles didn't mind her singing with the Firestreaks at first. The bass player was one of us, and they thought that it was good for her to *mix*. How could she learn to fit in and hide herself away, they reasoned, if she didn't mix?

Aunt Darya had a quiet word to her when it became obvious that she was sleeping with Ray McHale, the Firestreaks' lead guitarist, but she took that meekly and reasonably enough. Uncle Shilaq had us both on the carpet when we arrived home too stoned to know what day it was, but it was water off a duck's back. We knew it was all okay—and the aunts and uncles seemed to know it too, deep down. They were understanding people; they didn't tell us what not to do, the way Father John or Father Valentine would have done; they only told us to be careful. They didn't see any real problem in what Cecilie was doing with The Firestreaks.

After all, it was only music, only performing, and our kind are born to perform.

The alarm bells didn't begin to ring loudly until some time after the Firestreaks cut their first single, when it became a minor hit. A minor hit meant publicity, and the first rule of our existence is, of course, that all publicity is bad publicity and good publicity is worst. All of a sudden, Cecilie's photograph began to pop up here, there and everywhere in the newspapers, and she even made it on to the TV. Everybody watches TV, even in the frozen north.

When Father John and Father Valentine came down to see us it was obvious that they were hopping mad—and not just with Cecilie. Their real wrath was reserved for the aunts and uncles who'd let us "run wild". They knew it had to be the fault of the aunts and uncles because they took it for granted that it couldn't be theirs. They'd brought us up so carefully and so well, hadn't they?

In a way, facing them was fun, because it made us part of a conspiracy with adults—the aunts and uncles—for the first time in our lives. We looked upon the whole thing as a freak of nature, like a sudden storm, that had to be meekly endured while it was happening, but could be forgotten as soon as it went away. We listened stoically to Father Valentine's legendary lecture on the perils of fame, but we didn't really hear a word.

Father John wasn't quite so predictable, and I couldn't help being interested in some of what he said.

"These are bad times for our kind," he told us, soberly. "Things are changing far too rapidly. You're particularly vulnerable to the tide of change, because you're young, but you mustn't let yourself be seduced by visions of unlimited possibility. At the end of the day, there are only a handful of possibilities that really matter: survival or extinction; the long lazy afternoon or the coming of the Dark. The most difficult thing you have to learn in life is to keep a proper balance between hope and anxiety. It's an unpleasant lesson to learn that the proper balance has more anxiety in it than hope, but that's the way it is, and always will be."

I was still a sucker for a well-hung argument, but it didn't mean a thing to Cecilie. She was hooked on hope by now, and anxiety had been banished from her soul. She wanted to *live*. To her, at that particular moment in time, it seemed that only the humans really knew how to live, and not all of them: only the young humans; only the beautiful people.

Cecilie was already a beautiful person and then some; she had advantages mere humans didn't have. Surely it must have been one of us who invented the mini-skirt—human just don't have the legs for it!

* * * * * * *

The Firestreaks never reached the very top. Maybe it would have been better if they had, and maybe it was unjust that they didn't. Cecilie really did have a lovely voice, and Ray McHale was as competent a guitarist as many who achieved greater things, but they didn't have a real writer on the team, and they didn't get the kind of material that could sustain them for long. Personally, I think it was a bad career move to enter the Eurovision Song Contest, and a worse career move to come second, but that's life.

It was the infamous affair of the centerfold that really screwed things up. I never did discover how Father Valentine got hold of a copy; I'm pretty certain that none of the family had a subscription. If I had to bet on it, I'd hazard a guess that it was one of the men in the village who got the magazine, and his wife who gleefully recognized Cecilie in spite of all she'd done to alter her bodywork. Either way, it was the end, so far as the family was concerned. Father John came to fetch us home, and it was pretty obvious that, if and when we were put back into the network, we would probably be bound for Siberia or Patagonia.

I was surprised, and hurt, when it became clear that the mothers held me to blame for it all. They had allowed us to stay together so that Cecilie could exercise a benign influence upon me, and they naturally assumed that the influence had unfortunately flowed in the wrong direction. I pleaded my innocence in vain—but at least I had the sense to ride with the punches. Cecilie didn't.

Cecilie ran away.

100

She went back to London to live with Ray McHale, and she left a note to say that if anyone came after her, or tried to interfere with her chosen career, she'd complain to the police and the *News of the World*. The police probably wouldn't have taken any notice, but the *News of the World* certainly would—she was, after all, a fading pop-star who'd once posed in the nude for the kind of magazine they put on the top shelf at W. H. Smith's.

* * * * * * *

Cecilie wasn't ever any threat to our security—not really. She only wanted to live, after the fashion she'd adopted for her own. She was a product of the times: times when there really didn't seem to be any limits; times when joy and extravagance were sanctioned by everyone except *us*. Cecilie was only doing what all our kind have done ever since mankind first appeared: pretending to be human.

She just pretended a little bit too hard, that's all.

"No one will hurt her, will they?" I said to Father John, when it finally became clear that the break was absolute.

"This isn't America or the Dark Ages," Father John assured me. "We don't have cousins with daggers hidden in their long black cloaks. But there are worse things than being assassinated. She's cut off from the family, and the fact that she did it to herself won't make it any easier to bear when she needs us."

"When she needs us," I told him, "she'll come back. And we'll take her back, won't we."

"If it's as simple as that," he agreed, "yes we will. But if she really does become famous, she'll have to stay away. We can't stand too much scrutiny, you see. Our private lives are too different—it's difficult enough to cope with the village gossip and the government's data-gatherers."

The next time I saw Cecilie—the last time I saw her—I did my best to persuade her to drop it all. I knew it wasn't going to work, but I had to try. By then, she was a whore through and through. She had contrived to make herself even more beautiful, and she regarded her beauty as pure commodity. She'd left the Firestreaks and abandoned Ray

McHale, and she was determined to make it on her own, any way she could.

She did.

I suppose she isn't exactly a star, even today, but she's well on her way to being a household name. TV has made her face familiar to millions of people. She fits in to her chosen scene very well—as well she might, given that she had a lot of early practice in the dubious art of following convention.

I don't know how lonely she is, but I don't suppose it matters to her. Not much.

How many others are there just like her? I could name three, and guess at one or two others—but it's interesting, in a way, that there might be many more. Our kind are so good at hiding, at fitting in—nobody knows how many of us there are in Britain, or Europe, or the world.

Once, I wanted to write a science fiction story—this one strictly for our own consumption—about a future time in which human beings have become extinct but nobody knows, because the world is still ludicrously overpopulated with our lineages, all of them pretending fiercely to be human and defending their secret to the death, from *everyone*. I know it's silly, but...

I know that I have to forget the other stories, and concentrate on this one. I know that I have to finish it with a lesson—a *moral*—because that's the only hope I have of excusing the fact that I've written it. For what it's worth, though, those of my readers who are utterly horrified by the mere fact of its existence are over-reacting. If it were ever to fall into the hands of human beings, they'd just think it was science fiction, and pretty dull at that—not a monster or a mad assassin in sight.

The lesson we might try to learn, I think, is this: we've reached a threshold in our career as a species, and things will never be the same again. Even the Father Valentines of this world already know that, but it hasn't quite sunk in. They think of it all as decadence and corruption, but it isn't. The point is that the humans now have lots of things that are genuinely valuable, but which we're reluctant to share. It's not just medicine and the possibility of setting off on all the great science-fictional adventures, like conquering the universe and becoming immortal—I'm sure we'll figure out a way to jump on those bandwagons eventually. It's seemingly-trivial things like excitement and well-being and quality of life. We think we have those things already, by our own standards, but I'm not so sure.

I think that what we have to learn from my sister Cecilie, and all the others like her, is that there are some aspects of modern life that really have to be *lived* to be appreciated, and not just *performed*, hollowly, by way of imitation.

I'm not arguing that we should blow our cover and try to become full partners in Planet Earth Enterprises (Incorporated or otherwise). I'm not even saying that we should condone what my sister Cecilie's done, or copy the particular ambitions that drew her away from her family and her wider kin. I'm just saying that we ought to look a little longer and a little harder at what the humans of today are doing, and try to figure out what might be in it for us. If it's left to the humans, they'll only louse it up, but we could really do it *well*, if we were only prepared to try.

Maybe we could be really beautiful people if only we could loosen up a bit, and think a little more about living our lives and a little less about concealing them. Maybe that isn't such a silly and shabby ambition to have.

* * * * * * *

This story is dedicated to the bad; I have a sneaking suspicion that they'll be the only ones who can possibly understand.

RIDING THE TIGER

It had been a long and peaceful evening. I liked to work late in the lab, when everyone else had gone home. It was quiet, and it was lonely. Not that silence ever fell, or that the labs were ever entirely unpopulated—not my lab, anyhow; but there are special kinds of noises which humans make and there's a special kind of presence that humans have, and while I can hear those noises and feel that presence I can never quite relax.

The other sounds—the hum of machinery, the twittering of the birds, the spinning of the exercise-wheels in the mouse cages—had become a kind of music to me, a lullaby for my faint but constant anxieties. The physical presence of the animals was a comfort, even though the animals were simply aspects of my enquiries, mere instruments of my overt and covert researches.

I often worked late at the labs. You have to work more than twice as hard when the work you're supposed to be doing is really only a cloak hiding secret work which nobody shares.

When *he* came into the lab, all the comfort and contentment disappeared, just like that. They would have gone in an instant if he had only been human, but he wasn't—and that added an extra turn of the screw to the pitch of my anxiety. It's a sad fact that the presence of humans, intrinsically disturbing though it was, was less so than the presence of my own kind.

When I was young, and still in the bosom of my family, it had been very different; then, the presence of my own kind had always been reassuring, always a signal that everything was all right. Nowadays, I felt that I was in hiding from my own kind as well as the others—except, of course, that my own kind could always find me, if they really wanted to.

"Francis?" he said, not bothering to add the surname that I was currently using. He didn't immediately come forward. He was being polite, waiting for a reaction.

"I don't know you," I said, perhaps a little too coldly. I was sure of that, even though the mere fact that I'd never seen the face he was wearing didn't signify anything at all.

"No," he admitted. "The name I'm using at present is Vincent Napier." Still he kept his distance.

"You seem to know mine," I said, dryly.

"You're easy to identify," he said. "Easy to see, for those who have eyes. A teacher is always in the public eye. I'm not criticizing. It's easier to hide in the open, these days. Those of our kind who live as recluses are behind the times. But it'll always be easier for others to know who and where and what you are than for you to know them. And you know there's a risk involved in being what you are, don't you?"

"I know," I said. How could I not know, after the careful and closeted upbringing I'd had? I could still hear my father's voice, incessantly reminding me of the need to be invisible in the great human crowd.

Once upon a time, I'd harbored childish dreams of using my extra-human capabilities to become a famous sportsman—or a famous *anything*—but my father had made me feel so bitterly ashamed of those kinds of dreams that the dreams had shriveled and died. It seemed to me that a little bit of my soul had shriveled too. Mary had hung on to her childish dreams—Father was old-fashioned enough to think that it mattered far less what girls had inside their heads—but mine had perished. I learned never to talk about any of my later ambitions to the family, because I knew that they loved me far too much to let me keep them, and follow them, and become what I wanted to be.

When I left home, I left for good. So did Mary, but I was the greater disappointment of the two, at least to Father.

"I'm not your enemy, Francis," said he-who-was-presently-Vincent Napier. "I haven't come to call you to account, or even to find out what you're doing. In fact, I'm able to tell you that there are at least some interested parties who approve wholeheartedly of what you're doing, and would move to defend and protect you if...."

He left it there. Well, he would say that, wouldn't he? Whoever he was, whatever he wanted, he'd make that bid for my trusting attention. There was no point in my saying that his "interested parties" couldn't know what I was doing, or why. They could, and they probably did. They didn't have to send ingenious spies out to crack the codes protecting my data-discs; all they had to do was study the camouflage. Anyone who knew that I was doing secret research alongside the work I was publishing, and why, would be able to work out what kind of work it was. A glance round the lab, at the equipment and the animals, would probably have been enough to inform anyone who knew what the machines were for.

I wondered, though, whether he-who-was-presently-Vincent Napier did know what the machines were for. There are very few of our kind who know the first thing about science—any kind of science. My parents and others like them believed with all an unshakeable conviction that science is a *human* thing, and hence worthless, and that the awesome tradition of which *we* were the inheritors was infinitely finer. After all, they would say, hadn't our traditional wisdom served us well for literally millions of years? And what could biochemical genetics possibly have to teach those who knew the old songs?

Only everything, Father. Only everything.

"What do you want?" I said, flatly. There was nothing in my voice to welcome him, or to give him permission to approach a single step closer. I wanted him to go away. I wanted to be left alone, to the quiet unsilence and the peaceful absence of anything more intelligent than a cooing dove.

"Do you know a man named William Austerling?" he asked, softly.

I did know a man named William Austerling. Not a human man—one of our kind. Perhaps the only non-human man of *my* kind in the world. He was the only man of our kind I had been tempted to make contact with for five years. I would have, if he had not discouraged it. Austerling was, so far as I knew, the only other man of our kind engaged in serious research in biochemical genetics in the entire British Isles. If there were others, I knew nothing about them. If there were others, they didn't go to academic conferences like the one at which I had briefly met Austerling.

I'd been surprised to see him there, but only mildly—and in a way, I was disappointed not to see others. I hadn't been particularly surprised, or offended, when he'd made it clear that he wanted to keep his distance, at least for the time being. I understood how he felt. There had been nearly as much relief as discomfort in the knowledge that he didn't want to make contact yet.

"He heads a private research institute on Salisbury Plain," Napier added, misunderstanding my hesitation. "Partly funded by the Ministry of Defense, partly by...other sources."

"Other sources" was a delicate way of saying "some of us". There have always been some of us who've taken the precaution—purely for defensive purposes, of course—of becoming rich. Money doesn't attract attention, if you handle it carefully. Humans are not by nature a discreet species, but wealth imposes its own necessities. Humans have all kinds of ways of hiding money away, and there are those of us who accept that providence most gratefully.

For a moment, I envied William Austerling. All my money came from human sources. No man of my own kind had ever approached me, clandestinely, to say: "We think you ought to be encouraged, Francis. We'll supply any equipment you need."

"Did Austerling send you?" I asked. "Have you come to offer me a job?"

He permitted himself the faintest of smiles. "No," he said. "Although you might be able to get one, if that's what you want. You could have applied on your own account—but you didn't, did you?" He seemed to think that counted in my favor.

"I know Austerling," I said. "Why don't you come to the point?"

"I want you to smuggle me into his institute," he said. "I need to get in there without him knowing who or what I am. I want you to serve as my Trojan horse."

"How do you expect me to do that?" I said, almost as astonished by his assumption that I could as by his presumption that I might.

"You have a good reason for demanding to be admitted," he told me. "Your sister Mary is there, and her life is in danger. Austerling knows you, and if he wants to be difficult you can prove your identity to his satisfaction. If you turn up on his doorstep, he can't turn you away—and if you make enough fuss about getting in, they won't question your statement that the person with you is your father. They don't know your father, but they know *you* do."

I hardly listened to the latter phases of his Machiavellian reasoning. My thoughts were brought to a near-standstill by what he said about Mary.

I realized, guiltily, that I hadn't seen Mary for six months, and hadn't even noticed the fact. I hadn't seen her in the flesh for more like twenty years, but I hadn't seen her *at all* for six months. It's hard to notice an absence, especially from something as inherently uninteresting as TV, even more especially since she'd been reduced to doing ads and bit parts. Even so, I should have realized that she wasn't there. She was my sister, and for twenty years I'd been tracking the progress of her career. The mere fact that her career had been on the wane shouldn't have prevented me noticing her disappearance. The waning had seemed natural enough—she'd had to let her face age, even though her shapeshifting abilities could easily have maintained the appearance of youth. A mimic species has to be responsible even to the frailties of its model. Those of our kind who are in the public eye have to be very scrupulous about that sort of thing. I'd aged my own appearance while I'd been at the university.

"What's wrong with her?" I said, feeling my heart quiver with cold anxiety. I hadn't seen her for twenty years, but she was my sister, my only sibling. I had the kind of love for her that only individuals of our kind have, and the fact that I'd learned enough human science to be familiar with the logic of kin selection didn't devalue that love at all. *Why hadn't Austerling got in touch, given that he knew who and where I was?*

"Accidental poisoning," said Napier, too calmly by half. "Some new designer drug—she's always had a habit, Francis, as you probably know. Lately, with her career in the doldrums...she's got in deeper. Most psychotropics affect us much the same way as them, but this one seems to have been the exception. The word is that she nearly died, Francis. Somebody stepped in and took her to Austerling. He didn't know of any place else to take her. Austerling doesn't usually take medical cases, even emergencies involving our kind—but he was pressured into taking this one. Maybe it connects with his work in some way. Look Francis, I don't know about this, but she might be in more danger now than she was before Austerling took her in. You've every reason to demand access to her—and I hope that the fact that I'm telling you this, when Austerling wouldn't, is reason enough for you to meet my *quid pro quo*. I need to get in, Francis. We need to know for sure what he's doing there, because if he's doing what we think he's doing, it's something that involves us all—something that we all have a right to know about."

"Something dangerous," I said, almost off-handedly.

"Something dangerous," he echoed—and for the first time, he took one step closer. "You knew that when you started out in this line of work," he continued, quietly. "You knew that it was dangerous, in every possible way. You must have known, all along, that a time would come...and now it has. You can't stay out of it, Francis. Mary's involvement throws you in at the deep end, but even if there was nothing personal, you'd be involved. You took the decision to involve yourself a long time ago. Now, it's just a matter of which particular route you take to the centre of the maze. I know that you have no real reason to trust me, Francis, but you must know that you have no reason to trust anyone else—certainly not Austerling. All I can do is ask, Francis. Will you take me in with you? Will you let me pretend to be your father?"

I could have said no. I could have simply and flatly said *no*. But everything he said was true. I'd known from the very beginning that I'd elected to play with dynamite. A little knowledge is a dangerous thing; too much can easily be le-

109

thal. The only two things I knew about Vincent Napier were that he had come to tell me that my sister Mary was in danger, and that he wanted me to walk blindfold into the crossfire between two of the mysterious factions that constitute the freemasonry and the secret politics of our society—but as he said, it was all just a matter of which route I intended to take into the heart of the maze.

I'd been willing to talk to Austerling, to share what I knew—but he hadn't wanted to. He had cold-shouldered me...and now he had charge of my sister, and hadn't even taken the trouble to tell me she was ill.

"Do you have a car?" I asked.

"Yes," he said, "but we'll take yours. It'll be identifiable. Every little helps."

* * * * * * *

From that moment on, I was completely in his hands. At his direction I left a note for my lab assistant, saying where I'd gone and why. I also left a message on the professor's answerphone, giving the same information. I didn't phone my parents, in case my doing so somehow upset Vincent Napier's intended masquerade.

He was meticulous. He took the trouble to change his appearance so that he looked the way my father usually looked, even though we had no reason to suppose that anyone at Austerling's research institute had ever seen any member of my family. It couldn't be an exact likeness, because I hadn't seen Father in quite some time, but among our kind likenesses never are exact. One of the benefits of not being prisoners of our flesh is that none of our kind, at forty or any other age, has to wear the face he truly deserves.

As soon as we were on the road I started a cross-examination of sorts. I didn't expect to get very far, and I didn't, but I did get answers of a sort.

"What exactly is your job, Mr. Napier?" I asked, figuring that asking him who he was working for would be too easy to evade.

"I'm a soldier," he said. I thought at first he meant it metaphorically; I thought he was simply laying claim to being a humble functionary in one of the factions, but he wasn't. After the briefest of pauses, he went on: "I was in the Gulf last year, with what the newsreaders call the Special Forces. I've fought in every war since the big one."

"World War Two?" I said, incredulously.

"World War One," he corrected me. "At least that's what they call it now. At the time, it was the war to end war—the war to save civilization. For our kind, it was the *first* war—the first one we couldn't entirely avoid. Hundreds did, of course, but then even then we were beginning to be enmeshed in the nets of human bureaucracy. To continue to hide in their midst, at least in nations like this one, we had to be content to be recorded...and once you're recorded, and living a visible life, it's not so easy any more to change your identity. That war was the first war into which any substantial number of our kind were conscripted. We didn't all stay, of course...we were expert deserters, and one glimpse of Flanders fields must have been more than enough for most of those who got that far. But for those few of us who didn't run, for whatever reason, it was quite an experience. Men of our kind make good soldiers, Francis. We're difficult to kill, and our particular talents are quite an asset. There are several others in the SAS, more in the regiments, and quite a little cadre in MI5 and its shadowy analogues—not nearly as many as there used to be in the KGB, though. There are some places where the only way to be hidden from the watchers is to be among those who watch the watchers...but I suppose you must have guessed that."

"But why?" I asked, even though I knew it was a digression, a deflection away from more urgent questions, and even though I knew that was why he was probably telling me. I didn't have to expand the question. He knew perfectly well what I meant. Why fight in *their* wars? Why get caught up in *their* madness?

"Because we have to," he said. "In order to hide among them, we must do as they do—and the harder it becomes to hide, the more we have to do. We might think that their wars aren't our wars—most of us, I know, think exactly that—but their world is our world, and as long as we're content to remain mimics and fugitives, what *they* are determines what *we* can be. We can't just drift with the tides and current of human society, Francis; we have to be part of the processes which shape that society. Whether we like it or not, we have to be."

I saw then that his strategy was more subtle than I'd thought. He was deflecting me from the questions I really wanted answered, but he had led me to answers of a kind by a roundabout route. He wasn't giving a name to the faction that he represented—but what good would a name have been to a rank outsider like me, who knew next to nothing about the groups which aspired to steer the course of our private history? What he was doing instead was to explain a philosophy: a particular attitude to the complex relationship of human destiny and *our* destiny.

He was a soldier. He was prepared to bear arms for his cause, and his cause—his *true* cause—was the guidance of human history. In which direction, I wondered, was he trying to take it?

"Why do you want to get into Austerling's labs?" I asked, bluntly.

I was too blunt; he simply ignored the question. "I once heard a limerick," he said. "It goes:

"There was a young lady from Riga,
Who smiled as she rode on a tiger;
They came back from the ride
With the lady inside,
And the smile on the face of the tiger.

"It's a cautionary expansion of a neat little proverb, which your father undoubtedly taught you. *Who rides a tiger may never dismount.*"

I'd heard it, but not from my father. He was never that subtle. "So humankind's a tiger," I said, "and our kind is the rider. The tiger could swallow us up if we relaxed our control, and would feel very satisfied with itself if it did. What's it got to do with Austerling, or Mary, or me?"

Bluntness, alas, wasn't getting me anywhere.

"We weren't ready for the Great War," he said, airily. "In fact, we weren't ready for the twentieth century. We weren't even ready for the Industrial Revolution. The tiger's been out of control for two hundred years, Francis, and things are still getting worse. You of all people must know how difficult it will be to continue living in hiding, in a world where bureaucracy and science are growing apace. Before, I compared it to being caught in a net, but it's actually worse than that. I first realized what it was really like—what it would be like—when I was in France in 1917. That was where I first saw barbed wire. I lost count of the men who stumbled into the wire during night attacks, and got caught—wounded men, mostly. Men who died because they couldn't get clear, because the barbs were digging into their clothing and into their flesh, slowly tearing them apart. That's what's closing around us, Francis; that's what will trap us all, if we don't take care. Tangled and trussed by the wire, we'll be helpless—and if the tiger ever figures out that we exist, it will gobble us up."

"But what...?" I began again.

"...does it have to do with Austerling?" he finished for me. "Maybe nothing, Francis. To tell you the truth, we don't know what he's really working on. We know about the surface stuff—the work he does for the MOD—but we don't know about the *real* secrets. He and his masters are very close-mouthed about that. Just like you. Nothing odd about it, of course—secrecy is our whole way of life, our first instinct, our essential nature. The work we do know about— the work he's doing with and for the humans—is work on biological warfare. Where that fits into the politics of tiger-riding, your guess is as good as mine."

I thought about that for a moment while I negotiated a tricky double bend. When I'd come off the M4 it had begun to rain, and now we were way out into the wilds where there were no street-lights the visibility wasn't too good. I was driving just a little to fast for the conditions. I was in a hurry.

"It'd be a damn sight easier to ride a tiger," I commented, finally, "if the riders didn't devote so much of their time and imagination to squabbling among themselves."

"Everybody knows that," he admitted. "Unfortunately, everybody wants everybody else to back down and see the error of their ways. We've been fighting our own wars for a very long time, Francis—and you know what slaves we are to tradition."

I wondered about the wisdom of asking the next question, but in the end, I decided that there was nothing to be gained by leaving it unvoiced.

"How do you know that I'm not on Austerling's side?" I asked him. "How do you know that, if and when I find out what this is all about, I won't take his side against yours?"

"I don't," he said, as I should have known he would. "But it doesn't matter, does it? You probably won't even get to find out which side he's on—but if you do, and want to join it, good luck to you. I'll be long gone, hopefully without their ever realizing that I've been in. Sooner or later, I suppose, you'll have to decide what side you're on—if you don't volunteer, you'll be conscripted—but if I were you, I wouldn't be in any hurry."

I let more time go past, but not because I was mulling over his metaphorical conundrums. I had more practical matters to think about.

"How do you know that Mary's there?" I asked him, after a pause. I wondered whether the people he was working for might have put her there, just to set all this up, but it didn't seem very plausible.

"She's well-known," he said, shortly. "We steer clear of her, for exactly that reason, but we always keep an eye on people like her." He didn't say, "in case they become too visible" but I knew what he meant. "The drug thing was a touchy situation," he continued. "Touchy enough for someone to pull strings—even touchy enough for them to involve Austerling. We didn't cause this, Francis; it's just a window of opportunity. We can't be sure, mind you, that Austerling's people didn't cause it. If it *wasn't* an accident...."

He was very slick with the dangling sentences. Perhaps too slick. It was, after all, a performance he was putting on, to secure my co-operation It was even less plausible that Austerling's backers might have fed my sister some kind of poison, just to get her off the street, than that someone would do it to set up an opportunity to go in after her.

On the other hand, they hadn't called. Austerling knew who and where I was, but he hadn't called to tell me that my

114

sister was in bad trouble. Maybe he was just following his instincts, being discreet, but the fact remained. He'd have left me out in the cold, while my sister was fighting for her life.

There was a cold knot in my stomach, which grew tighter every time I thought about it.

* * * * * * *

The road that led to Austerling's research facility was narrow and winding, and it didn't even have cats'-eyes, but it brought us eventually to a pair of tall iron gates set in a brick wall. It wasn't a particularly intimidating brick wall, and it didn't seem at all out of place as it snaked way into the woods to either side. It was only ten or eleven feet high, with no broken glass or razor wire on top—but it was only a first line of defense.

"There are two more fences inside," Napier told me, offhandedly. "Carefully hidden in the bushes—both fitted with alarms. The house is set well back, of course. You'd need a helicopter to catch a glimpse of it."

I got out of the car. The headlights spread enough illumination to show me the telephone mounted on the gatepost, and the camera mounted above it. The camera had already moved to fix its electronic gaze on my face before I picked up the phone, but the searchlight didn't come on until I pressed the buzzer set beneath the cradle.

I didn't stand on ceremony. "This is Francis Marlow," I said, giving the surname by which I was known at the university. "My father's with me. You've got my sister Mary here, and we want to see her. We want to see her *now*." I didn't have to feign the indignation or the determination.

"This is a restricted area, sir," said a voice at the other end, which might or might not have been human. "I'm afraid I can't let you in. If you care to leave an address where we can contact you, we'll get in touch in the morning."

"The hell you will," I said. "You'll get Austerling, *now*. We want to see her, *now*—and we also want to know why he didn't tell us she was here. If we aren't admitted, and if we don't get a satisfactory explanation, I'm going to ask some very awkward questions, *in public*."

He didn't even bother to argue. "Please wait a few moments, sir," he said. "I'll see if Dr. Austerling's available."

Dr. Austerling, it transpired, was available. Even at two o'clock in the morning, he was available.

"Dr. Marlow," he said, when he came to the phone. "We have met, I believe."

Swiftly and succinctly, without waiting to be asked, I told him when and where we'd met, and just enough of what had passed between us to assure him that I was who I said I was. "That's why," I finished, grimly, "I find it so difficult to understand why you didn't take the trouble to tell me that my sister was here. My father and I don't appreciate the fact that the family had to find out indirectly, from a third party."

"I'm sorry about that," he said, smoothly. "I'm afraid that security can become habit-forming. I rather envy you the opportunity to work in a public institution, free of all the red tape that plagues us here. I'll have a word with the Head of Security—I'm sure he'll permit you to enter, under the circumstances."

Several minutes dragged by while some mysterious process took its course within the facility. Then a third voice came on the line, brusquely telling me to get back in the car and wait for the gates to open. I did so, with alacrity, unable to suppress a small pang of triumph over the ease with which I'd fooled them.

The gates opened, and closed again behind us. Our path through the woods was brightly lit by lamps which had come on when the gates opened, but we could see nothing to either side—all the beams were directed on to the winding roadway.

When I finally pulled up in front of the main building we had three spotlights shining at us; it was impossible to judge how big the house was or how many other buildings there might be. Austerling was waiting for us on the steps, with a uniformed man at his side, who I took to be the Head of Security. I was slightly surprised that the uniformed man was a human, but only slightly. It might be ironically easy, I supposed, to keep secrets from a Head of Security.

116

Napier hung back while I went forward, claiming the full attention of the waiting men. I knew that wouldn't seem odd, even though he was supposed to be the father and I the son. I was a man of the world, and he—supposedly—was just some tradition-bound stick-in-the-mud from way up north.

"What's wrong with her?" I said, without ceremony. "Don't beat about the bush—I'm not a medical doctor but you know full well that I can understand all the words."

Austerling's eyes spoke volumes, and what they said, boiled down to its essentials, was: *not in front of the human.* I already knew that whatever had happened to Mary had something to do with our particular nature, but I wasn't about to be fobbed off with that kind of appeal.

"We really don't know, Dr. Marlow," Austerling began, all the while begging me with his body-language to bear with him. I made a dismissive gesture with my hand as I climbed the steps.

"Where is she?" I demanded.

Austerling turned to the security man, as if to say: "You see how it is—what can I do?" The security man stepped forward, as if he intended to take over, but I cut him off before he was half way into his first word.

"I don't give a damn about your rules and regulations," I said, looking him straight in the eyes. "We don't want to hear about security clearances or any other crap like that. You had no right to bring her here, but now she is here you have no right to keep us away from her. If you don't want us around your lousy germ warfare labs, then you'd better ship my sister out to some NHS hospital where we don't have to go through all this shit to get to see her, okay?"

The security man was probably about to protest that he didn't want Mary here any more than he wanted me here, but it was Austerling's turn to cut him off.

"I'm truly sorry about all this, Ned," he said, invoking all the authority and balm of his best bedside manner. "I know it seems as though one irregularity is leading to another and yet another, but I'll take full responsibility. I'll square everything with the Department—you have my word on it. Please bear with us."

It wasn't quite the end, but it was the decisive move. The security man was annoyed, but he backed off after a bit of token blustering, and Austerling left him standing as he hustled us through the main doors and into the hallway. He didn't pause there—he hurried us along a side-corridor and up a flight of stairs. All his attention was still fixed on me—nobody had spared poor "Father" a second glance.

"Tell me," I insisted, once we were clear of the human. "No bullshit—I want to know."

"To tell you the truth," he said, with a heartfelt sigh, "I'd be glad of a second opinion. It's something I've never seen before. Apparently, the stuff she took is some new synthetic drug—I really don't know anything about that sort of thing, but the people in London who panicked say that there's a whole series of them coming through on to the market...it's supposed to be a mild hallucinogen, and that's all it is, for humans. Toxic, of course, but not in low doses. Our kind shouldn't play with things like that—we really shouldn't. We need our presence of mind, always. Even alcohol...but that's not the point. This isn't just a matter of lowered inhibitions...somehow, this drug went straight to the chemistry of the mechanism by which we consciously direct our mimicry. It screwed up the whole process. It was the change itself that panicked our people, Francis, but that's not the whole of it. She's lost her ability to change. It looks bad, and we're not making any headway...."

We arrived at the room where Mary was. Austerling paused, looking both ways down the corridor before taking a key from his pocket. There was nobody about but us. For the first time he looked directly at Napier—but not suspiciously. He had not the slightest notion that Napier was anyone but who I said he was. Again, I felt a slight surge of triumph—no guilt at all, even though I hadn't the slightest idea what Napier had come here to do.

"I'm sorry, sir," said Austerling, with awkward formality. "This is going to come as a shock."

Napier nodded, gravely. He looked for all the world like a father, anxious for his offspring.

Austerling turned the key in the lock and opened the door. He preceded us through it. I stayed back to close it, gripped by reflexive politeness.

I don't think Napier had to feign the gasp of alarmed surprise he let out when he saw the sleeping form of what was supposed to be his daughter. I didn't have to feign mine.

I'd heard, as we all do, that the kinds of faces you pull as a kid, trying to test the limits of grotesquerie, are nothing by comparison with the kinds of changes that *can* overtake you, if you really lose control and your hind-brain sets out to display the secrets buried away in our evolutionary heritage. I'd always thought of those stories as something made up purely for the purpose of training kids to be careful; now, I wasn't so sure.

Mary looked like something out of an old sci-fi movie. It was as if she was wearing a rubber lizard-man face-mask, shaped for nightmare effect. She didn't look real any more; she looked like something inert, something nightmarish. But she was breathing.

It wasn't a mask, of course.

I hadn't realized. Somehow, I had just taken it for granted that she'd be lying there looking the way she always did—unconscious, possibly surrounded by life-support equipment, but still *herself.* "Accidental poisoning," Napier had said. "She's lost her power to change," Austerling had added. There had been no way I could put two and two together and imagine *this*.

Suddenly, it became abundantly clear why Austerling had been anxious about what I might say in front of the uniformed man.

"Has that security man...?" I began, dazedly.

"Of course not," said Austerling. "The only humans who *did* see her, mercifully, think it was a hallucination. Now you know why the people who brought her here panicked—and now you know why I didn't dare turn her away. We have to find out how to counter this drug, Francis. For all our sakes."

I touched the skin of my sister's face, gingerly. It felt like the skin of some huge, obscenely-bloated snake, made of soft and silky-leathery scales. She didn't wake up.

"Why didn't it just wear off?" I whispered. "Surely she's metabolized the stuff by now, or excreted it. It can't be permanent. It can't be."

"We're in unknown territory," said Austerling, bitterly. "Dangerous territory, too. Ned's security works both ways, you know—he's supposed to watch me as well as keeping the world at bay. We're in trouble here, Francis. There are only twenty of our kind here, and more than fifty of theirs. You can't begin to understand what's at stake here, and how hard it is to maintain one secret organization within another. I'm sorry we didn't inform you, but we simply didn't dare. You do understand that, don't you?"

I nodded, dumbly. I could see why he'd been reluctant, and why I hadn't had as much reason as I supposed to be angry about it.

"But I really am glad that you found out," he went on. "On this one, I'll take all the help I can get. She does wake up occasionally, but she's not...well, you'll see in due course. There's no point waking her now. She can't speak, and she doesn't seem to understand what anyone says to her. You can stay with her if you want, but I'd like you to look over the test results. I can't show them to any of my human colleagues, you see, and...well, maybe you can think of something that we haven't tried. I'd be grateful if you could. Maybe you know something we don't...."

He didn't have to explain his vagueness about what I might know. I was a loner. Nobody knew exactly what I was working on, exactly what I might have discovered. He knew how very unlikely it was that I'd be able to help, but he also knew that he couldn't entirely rule out the possibility.

"You go," said the man who was pretending to be my father. "I'll stay with her." I'd almost forgotten him. He got the tone of voice exactly right: shock, grief, pain, paternal dignity...it was all in there. I knew, of course, that what he really wanted was a chance to get on with his own secret mission, but I didn't care. I knew as well as Austerling did how unlikely it was that any of my expert knowledge could be brought to bear on this particular enigma, but I couldn't rule out the possibility either. And I knew full well that this had become an urgent problem for everybody.

There was no way Mary could be permitted to stay this way forever, or even for long, whether she was here or anywhere else. If she couldn't change back to human form, Austerling would have no alternative but to kill her, and I'd have no alternative but to let him. All my life my family had thought me indiscreet, but I understood the absolute boundaries as well as anyone. We didn't dare let the humans know that there were monsters in their midst. They would turn on us like tigers, gobble us up, and smile with relief and satisfaction.

"You'd better show me everything," I said to Austerling, "as quickly as you can."

As we left, he turned to my fake father and said: "I'm afraid I'll have to lock you in."

Napier didn't even turn around. He just shrugged off the irrelevancy, and kept his eyes fixed on that dreadful face, for all the world like a father stricken dumb by horror and misery. Austerling couldn't possibly have doubted, even for a moment, that he understood the significance of that fatalistic shrug—but he didn't.

I did, but I didn't care. I was no longer concerned with Vincent Napier's secret mission; I had a much more urgent mission of my own.

* * * * * * *

I studied the documents that Austerling handed to me with minute care.

There was an analysis of the drug that Mary had taken. The people who'd brought her in had seized a substantial sample, and Austerling's people had investigated its biochemistry as thoroughly as they were able. There were also the results of a whole battery of physiological tests to which they'd subjected Mary.

I understood it all well enough, but I couldn't see anything in it that pointed to an obvious solution to the problem, or even a real explanation of what had happened.

When I was sure that I had the complete picture in my head I laid the documents down again on Austerling's leather-topped desk. He was sitting behind the desk, patiently watching me. His expression was bleak, but there was an evident glimmer of curiosity in his gaze. I remembered that I must be as much a mystery to him as he was to me. He hadn't dared to strike up an acquaintance at the conference, but he had a better opportunity now to find out how much I knew, and what kind of work I was doing at the university. He was understandably intrigued.

"It's only a temporary glitch," I said, desperate to believe it. "The metabolic mechanism is jammed, but it can be freed again, if only we can kick-start it, or supply the right kind of oil. It's just a matter of working out how."

He nodded. Neither of us wanted to waste time discussing the possibility that what had happened to Mary might be permanent and irredeemable. If that were so, it wouldn't be just a personal tragedy—the future of our species would be under threat.

It was up to us to find a way out, and quickly.

"The drug's intended effect—and its actual effect—is to interfere with neurotransmission," I said, slowly. "According to your analysis, it promotes the kind of quasi-random firing that's usually responsible for hallucinogenic sensory distortions, and it also excites the dopamine system, so that there's a simultaneous euphoric high. But your tests show that her serotonin levels are abnormally high—that's surely the wrong way round?"

"Not necessarily," said Austerling. "We have rather better homoeostatic mechanisms than humans do. Mary's system reacted to the dopamine boost by producing a compensatory increase in serotonin—and for our kind, that was normal. The high would have disappeared fairly quickly, but the hallucinations would probably have continued, at least for a while. I think the problem developed afterwards. Either something happened to the dopamine system itself as a result of the drug's effect—cell damage of some kind—or...."

He left the sentence dangling, like bait. He wanted to see if I could pick up the ball. I could see where he was pointing. According to the textbooks we'd both read, the third important protein in the human cycle was norepinephrine, the chemical that imprinted the cellular "memory" of dopamine-reward and serotonin-sensitivity, but I had no idea whether we were significantly different—or, if so, how.

I felt that I had to improvise, partly just to prove myself to Austerling but mainly because I knew that he'd already tried to solve the problem and failed. If I could come up with something he hadn't thought of, we might be up and running.

"Or the feedback system's been thrown out," I said, slowly. "She can't restore her own dopamine levels, and she can't activate the theriomorphic mechanism, maybe for the same reason. Have you tried injecting dopamine?"

"Yes," he said. "We also tried its immediate metabolic precursor, to see if we could reactivate the metabolic cycle at an earlier stage. Nothing."

"The trouble is," I went on, still speaking very slowly, to give myself a chance to think it out as I went, "if it's the norepinephrine that's screwed up, we can't compensate externally. It's not the quantity of norepinephrine that's vital to the work it does—it's the location of the effect. If the neuronal pathways that enable her consciously to change her appearance have been blocked because the norepinephrine's fouled up, it isn't easy to see how we might unblock them."

"How much do you know about the differences between our brain chemistry and theirs?" he asked.

"Nothing at all," I admitted. "As you must have deduced, I've been tracking the genetic differences between our kind and theirs, but I've been forced to concentrate entirely on the somatic cells. I only have one experimental subject of our kind to work with, you see—and that limits the kind of tissue-samples I can readily obtain."

At another time, the faint irony might have prompted a smile, but he just nodded.

"You know, of course, that we're not particularly closely related to humans, biologically speaking?" he said.

"I'd worked that out," I agreed. "According to the genes, we're about as closely related to humans as rats are. I figure that our line might have diverged from theirs as early as the Jurassic—the mimetic imperative didn't begin to bring us back into line until the Eocene, a hundred million years later. By that time, we'd evolved our own idiosyncratic versions of almost all the major proteins. The first time one of our kind is tested for a genetic fingerprint he's going to show up like a flaming beacon. The neurotransmitters are so basic and so specific in function that there shouldn't be a lot of difference across the entire mammalian spectrum—but then, we're rather special, aren't we? I know that our somatic cells have extra neuronal networks and extra cellular subsystems that allow us to change, but I don't know the first thing about what happens at the brain end. Do you?"

"A little," he confessed, "but not enough. You're right about norepinephrine being very important, but in *our* brains it doesn't work alone. There's some kind of secondary cell-memory system, which seemingly preserves a set of basic templates for our shape-shifting abilities. Nowadays, of course, we draw upon the human template almost exclusively—but the others are still there, and by no means atrophied. Our aging process inhibits our facility for change, and it also tends to favor a gradual reversion to more primitive templates. The ones we see in our old folk aren't far removed from the human, but there may be older templates locked away at the biochemical level. Perhaps there's even a saurian one. If there is, we've lost—or perhaps never had—the ability to draw upon it consciously, but it might still be effective if given the right biochemical stimulus. That's the hypothesis I've been working on. The question is, how do we persuade the archetype to disappear, given that we don't actually know how the extra system—I call it para-norepinephrine for convenience—actually works?"

I thought about it for a few seconds, looking down all the while at the useless papers on the desk, which told us everything except what we really needed to know.

"You say she's conscious sometimes?" I said, dubiously. Her mental state wasn't recorded; the documents dealt entirely with matters of physiology.

"Conscious but not at all coherent," he confirmed. "She seems to be in a constant state of terror—but given her serotonin levels, that's not entirely surprising. Dopamine calms her, but only for a while. She doesn't seem to be able to speak, or to understand speech."

124

I thought about that for a few seconds, and about the fact that Austerling's people hadn't even thought it worth recording.

"We don't actually know that the problem is biochemical at all," I said, pensively. "It could be psychological. The high serotonin levels might be a consequence rather than a cause."

"That's a distinction without a difference," he said, dismissively. "We're at the interface where psychology and physiology meet. We're not talking about some little Freudian glitch here—some repressed guilt that only surfaces in disturbing dreams, or some petty neurosis based in her uneasy relationship with her father. We aren't human, Francis. We don't have those kinds of hang-ups."

He spoke with open contempt, as my real father might have spoken—as nine out of ten of us would have spoken. But I wasn't so sure. I wasn't at all certain that we couldn't and didn't suffer from the same kinds of hang-ups as humans. I thought about my own life, and the way I'd followed Mary into voluntary exile...and then I thought about the way that Napier had talked while we drove down, about the business of war and the tactics of tiger-riding.

"Maybe," I said, "it wasn't some unforeseen neurochemical effect at all. Maybe—just maybe—it was the particular hallucination she suffered when the psychotropic hit. Maybe she *dreamed* that she was *something different*, and maybe the dream caught her up and wouldn't let her go."

The more I thought about it, the more it seemed to make sense. I knew how easy it is for scientists to fall in love with their own hypotheses, but even so, I felt that I was on a better and more hopeful track than the one Austerling had been following. I had to hope so, because it as the only track I could see which led to a possible solution.

Maybe, I thought, the kind of life that Mary had elected to live among humans—deliberately cut off by her own kind—had finally come to the point where it was unbearable, and quite insupportable. Maybe, even if only subconsciously, she wanted out. Maybe the drug, just by lowering her inhibitions, had given her an opportunity to express that wish to get out, as extremely as possible, at the cellular level. Because our kind had evolved consciousness and intelligence in parallel with humans, we'd obtained conscious control over our ability to mimic humans—but maybe we retained, in our collective *subconscious*, the ability to make much grosser changes.

"You say she's not coherent," I continued, aloud, "and that she isn't able to speak. Maybe that's because she threw away the ability to speak human-fashion, and even the ability to think human-fashion. But maybe...just maybe...all we have to do is *reach* her, and make her understand what it is that she's done to herself."

"You think we can *talk* her out of this?" said Austerling, incredulously. But the contempt wasn't quite as strong as it had been before. Hope was beginning to thrust it aside. He wasn't yet ready to believe that I was right, but he could see that if I turned out to be right, then the implications for the future of the species might not be so bleak after all.

"I don't think *we* can talk her out of it," I said, permitting myself a slight sneer of my own. "But I think *I* might. I'm her brother. If anyone can get through to her, it's me. At least it's worth a try."

He hesitated, but then he nodded. "Okay," he said. I was already beginning to work out how I'd have to handle it, and what I'd have to say.

"There's one thing I'll need," I said.

When I told him what it was, he looked impatient, as if he thought that my sense of melodrama was getting the better of my scientific judgment—but then he shrugged, and found me what I wanted.

"If you're right," he said, as we went back along the corridor, "the problem might already have been taken care of. Your father may have done the job while we were talking."

I didn't reply to that. If my father was doing a job, he'd be far away from Mary's room by now. I knew full well, in fact, that our returning might blow the lid off whatever it was he'd come to do—but I'd only promised to get him in; I hadn't promised to buy him time. I wanted to get on with the work that *I* had come to do. If Napier was out of the way, I thought, so much the better.

126

At first, when Austerling unlocked the door of Mary's room to let us back in, I thought I'd been wrong about Napier. The chair in which he'd been sitting when we left was still occupied, and the person in it was wearing the clothes that Napier had worn. But the illusion couldn't last, even though the man had his back to us.

The way he was sitting was all wrong, and he certainly wasn't asleep.

"What the hell?" said Austerling, explosively.

He took three strides forward, taking hold of the sitter's head and twisting it so that he could look into the face.

It was a human face, and its humanness wasn't any mere pretence.

It was the security man Austerling had addressed as Ned, and he was dead. His neck had been broken.

I felt sick, because I hadn't expected it, and because I knew that I ought to have. I'd simply assumed that no damage would be done, and I'd had no right to assume any such thing.

Austerling looked back at me, his face desperate with anger and despair, and I began to realize at last the true magnitude of my offence.

"You stupid fool!" he said. "What have you *done*, you stupid bloody *fool*?"

* * * * * * *

There was a gun on the dead man's lap, and underneath the gun there was a note. Austerling picked them both up, scowled at the words which were neatly printed on the paper, and then handed to message to me. He kept the gun.

HE LET HIMSELF IN AS SOON AS YOU'D GONE, said the note. I HADN'T ANY CHOICE. SORRY.

If it was true, then Napier had killed the security man for Mary's sake, and for my sake, and for Austerling's sake, and for the sake of the Great Secret, as well as for his own. *If* it was true. It probably was. On the other hand, if I hadn't come storming in the way I had, maybe the security man's curiosity about what Austerling was hiding in here wouldn't have overflowed.

"Who is he?" Austerling demanded, having obviously worked out that Napier wasn't my father, and feeling a little sick about being taken for a mug. He wasn't exactly pointing the gun at me, but the *rapport* we'd established had definitely turned sour.

"I don't know," I said.

"*Where* is he?"

I shrugged, helplessly. If I'd been human, I'd have blushed. The fact that I didn't know the answers to the questions suddenly seemed very embarrassing indeed. I hadn't anticipated murder, but now that murder had been done, I knew that I was an accessory. I'd never been one of those who feel that killing humans is no worse than slaughtering cattle or swatting flies, but even if I had, I'd have been compelled to recognize that *this* murder was also an act of outrageous indiscretion, and had to be reckoned a truly heinous crime.

Austerling, his face ugly with wrath, plucked the receiver from the phone beside the bed. I got the impression that he was still making up his mind about what to say and do while he lifted the instrument to his mouth.

"It's Austerling," he said. "I'm in the girl's room. There's an intruder on the premises—one of ours. He's wearing Kelly's face and uniform. Kelly's dead. Don't sound the alarm; this is our business. Stop him if you can—kill him if necessary—but don't let the humans find out what's happening. Pass the word. Make sure all of our people know the score. And send someone up here to take care of Kelly's body."

Mary stirred in her sleep, moaning slightly, as if she were trying to wake up. But she didn't wake up. Whatever her dream was, she was its prisoner. It wasn't letting go.

It really is a dream, I told myself, trying to force my attention back to the real issue. *That's what I have to fight. Not some mysterious para-norepinephrine; just a bad dream.*

When Austerling put the phone down he turned back to me. His face was still pale, but it was under control. Even among ourselves, we know only too well how to prevent our features mirroring our inner selves. The gun in his hand was pointed at the floor.

"Why?" he asked. I had to admire the way he'd worked it all out—not only what had happened, but what to do about it. He was a quick thinker, when it came to matters he understood, and he didn't bother to repeat questions to which he wasn't going to get any answers. He always moved on.

"*Quid pro quo*," I said, with another slight shrug. "You should have told me about Mary. He convinced me that you were hiding her—implied very delicately that you might have sinister plans for her. I didn't have time to check his credentials, even if I knew who to check them with, or who he really is. You can probably guess who he might be better than I could."

He shook his head. Despite his self-control, the desolation showed through. He knew that he might lose everything, if our own people couldn't keep the humans in the dark. If his relationship with the Ministry of Defense was compromised, his secret masters might have to pull him out and relocate him—or maybe close him down for good."

"You," he whispered. "You, of all people. You're probably the only person in England who understands what I'm trying to do—and the necessity of doing it."

"And *vice versa*," I said. "But that didn't stop you freezing me out when we met. You must have checked me out. You knew exactly why I was on my own, outside the community. You decided to let things be—and when Mary was dumped on you, your instinct was still to leave me out of it. You should have told me."

It wasn't until I spoke that I realized just how much bitterness I had stored up. I realized that there was more to my own actions than I'd thought, and what a ready-made sucker I had been for the line that Napier had spun me. I realized how glad I'd been to be given a chance to hit back at Austerling and all that Austerling represented: my exclusion from every faction, every supportive network of our kind. I realized just how much I'd envied Austerling, his secretly-funded research establishment, and the approval that the makers and movers of our kind had bestowed upon him and not on me.

There was a knock at the door, and he pushed past me to answer it. I went to Mary's side, sitting down on the bed because I was too squeamish to disturb the corpse slumped in he chair. I reached out to try to shake her awake, determined to ignore what was going on behind me.

Having checked out who it was, Austerling opened the door to let in two men. They were both big men, and very muscular. When our kind go in for physical culture they make good use of heir natural advantages. These men were part of the security team within the security team. I don't know what effect they had on the humans, but they certainly scared me. One of them came forward to inspect the body while the other stayed with Austerling.

"Who is he?" asked the newcomer. He didn't mean the body, or me.

"I don't know," said Austerling, dully. "He doesn't, either—or says he doesn't. Do you know anything at all, Dr. Marlow?"

There wasn't any reason not to tell them what little I knew. I didn't owe any loyalty to anyone. I turned back briefly, and said: "He's using the name Vincent Napier. I think he's in the SAS—or was until recently. I don't know one faction from another, but he talked a lot about the need to control the humans. He spoke of our situation as riding a tiger, and he seemed to feel some sense of urgency about the possibility of the ride coming to an uncomfortable end in the very near future. He didn't say what he wanted here."

The phone rang, and I picked up the receiver reflexively before it was unceremoniously snatched from my hand by the man who was inspecting the body. "Fisher," he said, curtly. After listening for half a minute he put the instrument down again.

"He's gone," he said, shortly. "He didn't even try for any of the infectious agents. It wasn't the germ-cultures he was after, or anything to do with the hidden program. He's got the new immunoserum, though—the papers too. All the stuff relating to Diwaniya."

"We can replace the paperwork," said Austerling. "Can you cover it up? Can you...oh, *shit!*"

The expletive was a response to the sound that had interrupted him: the wail of sirens. As he swore he glanced sideways at the man beside him, who shook his head.

"It must be him," said Fisher. "He's cutting his way out. But we haven't lost yet—the humans will assume that it's someone coming *in*. If we send them out to search the grounds they won't catch him, and we'll have a chance to cover things up. It'll be touch and go, but...."

"Do it," said Austerling, shortly. "Leave the body. It's too risky to take it out now. Kelly will have to disappear into thin air. I don't want him found in those clothes, and his disappearance will add to the smokescreen. There's still just a chance that we might come through this. The Foundation won't be pleased about the immunoserum—but at the end of the day, that's of very marginal importance to our own work."

Fisher grunted, and looked down at Mary, who was still stirring in her sleep, but still not awake.

"What about her?" he demanded.

"Leave her too," said Austerling. "Francis has an idea. As the hallowed cliché has it, it's a long shot but it might just work. If it does, we can smuggle them both out alive. If it doesn't...."

He looked at me as he left that one dangling. I didn't bother to tell him that I'd prudently left word where I'd be. Things had got beyond the point where minor indiscretions counted for much. If the threat was seriously meant, and they really did have to contemplate disposing of both of us, they wouldn't worry about the people at the university asking questions. I couldn't quite bring myself to believe that they really did mean it, and that they really would kill us both if my idea didn't work out, but it wasn't something I wanted to brood on. There were more important matters in hand.

Deliberately, I turned my back on all of them. My hand was still on Mary's shoulder, and I began shaking her—not too vigorously, but with increasing insistence.

Fisher and his companion went out again, but Austerling stayed. He locked the door behind them, and I could feel his gaze upon me. I didn't bother to wonder how much hostility there was in his stare. My predicament was simple enough. If I was right about Mary's problem being psychological, and if I could break down the barrier she'd erected between herself and the human world which had swallowed her up entire, we'd be all right. Everything would be all right. It didn't matter what kind of panic was raging outside; my part was here.

Then her eyes opened, and it seemed that my heart stopped.

* * * * * * *

Mary's eyes weren't human eyes. They were like the eyes of a snake: vivid yellow, with lenticular pupils. They fixed themselves upon me as though they were the eyes of a cobra intent on fascinating a bird. I had to tell myself that I didn't mind, that it was what I wanted, that it was good that she should look at me in that fearsome way. I felt my heart lurch, but it was still beating.

I wanted her to stare at me. I wanted her to fix her attention upon me. It would help.

"Mary," I said, softly. "It's me. It's Francis."

I didn't have to change my face very much. Hardly at all, in fact. Unlike her, I'd always worn the same features. I'd never tried to become unusually handsome. The only thing I had to do to recover the appearance of the golden years we'd spent together was to ease away the false signs of aging.

She opened her mouth, but all that came out were inarticulate grunts. She couldn't revert mentally the way she'd reverted physically. She had no templates in her brain for long-extinct cultures and long-extinct languages. All she could do was grunt like an animal in pain, a forlorn creature which had lost touch with its species and its true identity.

"I know you can understand me," I said to her. "Whether you're conscious of it or not, you can understand what I'm saying. You know who I am, if you'll only let yourself remember. It's Francis, Mary. You remember me. You know who I am.

"I've come to tell you that it's over, Mary. The exile, the ostracism. It's over. You can come home with me, and live with me, for as long as you like, and as long as you need. They'll never separate us again, Mary, not now. It's all over, and it's time to start again. You know that, don't you? You know that it's time to start again. Your brain knows...your body knows...but this isn't the way, Mary. You have to take control. You have to decide what you want to be.

"You have to get your voice back, and your face. Do you remember what a beautiful voice you had, Mary? Do you remember how proud Father and Mother used to be of your voice? Do you remember how you used to sing the old songs, by the fireside, in the dead of winter when the snow was on the moors? Do you remember how happy we were? I was happy too, Mary, even though I was always getting things wrong, always being indiscreet. I couldn't sing the way you could, Mary, but I always loved listening to you. I always loved listening to you."

She tried to say something. She really did try. But all that came out were grunts. I heard Austerling move, adjusting his position. He didn't say anything, but I knew he was thinking about norepiphrenine and para-norepiphrenine, about some kind of vicious chemical truth drug, which could take away our magical powers and reveal us for the monsters we are. This was a bad night for him.

"I know that you can hear me, Mary," I said. "I probably sound strange, because your ears are playing tricks on you, but I know that you know who I am. You see, you're playing tricks on your ears, and on your voice, and on your face. You're playing tricks on yourself, but you really don't have to go on with it now. You can stop now, because everything's okay. I'm here, and I'm going to take you home with me.

"You can stay with me forever, if you want to. I'll never leave you again. You'll sing to me, the way you used to sing to all of us. In fact, we'll go back to see the family this winter. We'll all be together again, just the way it used to be. Do you remember what a beautiful voice you had, Mary? Do you remember what a beautiful face you had? I'm going to show you something now, Mary—and I don't want you to be frightened. I don't want you to be frightened, because it really isn't anything to be frightened of. All you have to do is remember, Mary. All you have to do is remember who and what you are. That's all. If you remember, everything will be all right."

I'd done everything I could. I lifted up the thing I'd asked Austerling to give me: the mirror that would reflect her intimidating gaze straight back into her terrible eyes.

I felt like Perseus confronting Medusa, and wondered whether we were in any way responsible for the origin of that myth. We probably were. We seem to have been responsible for most of the others.

Mary looked at herself in the mirror, and she screamed.

In spite of what I'd said, she was horrified and terrified—but that didn't matter. That didn't matter at all. The fact that she could scream was itself a seed of hope. She wouldn't have screamed if she hadn't been able to see. She wouldn't have screamed if she hadn't been able, consciously or subconsciously, to understand.

I knew when she screamed that I was right. The drug had only been the facilitator, not the cause. She'd done this to herself. She'd erased her own humanity, because she simply couldn't bear to be human any more, cut off by her family and her species. She'd simply reached the end of her tether, and the drug had set her nightmares free.

Once upon a time, I remembered, I'd thought that our kind might be really beautiful people, if we'd only loosen up and let ourselves go, if we'd only condescend to take heed of what the humans had learned about the way to live. But that had been back in the sixties, when the human world was a brighter place. It was the nineties now, and dead of night. Now, the battle wasn't to be beautiful. Now, the battle was simply to be less ugly.

While I watched her hideous face, its reptilian lines began to soften. The eyes changed first, but the skin was already softening, already losing its dreadful color. The process would take hours to complete, but once it had begun, I knew that nothing was going to stop it.

I lowered the mirror, and she closed her eyes. For a second or two I felt a stab of anxiety, in case the process might go into reverse, but it didn't.

I had been right and Austerling had been wrong. The chemistry was consequence, not cause. It was over. The bad trip had come to an end. She was coming back to reality.

I looked round at Austerling. He shrugged his shoulders very slightly, and nodded even more slightly, in grudging acknowledgement.

"You should have called me," I said, still feeling that I had to make it clear. "You could have saved yourself a lot of trouble."

"So it seems," he said. "I'll just have to hope that it all works out for the best. Maybe it will. Maybe your friend Napier has done us all a favor. Maybe I should have called *him* too, and made him a present of what he wanted."

"What was it he took?" I asked, not for a moment believing that he'd tell me.

"Not what you thought," he retorted. "You thought he wanted something of ours, didn't you? You thought he wanted some terrible secret that I'd discovered about our nature, our genes. Well, he doesn't give a damn about our secrets-within-the-secret. He was only interested in the work we're doing for the MOD—the biological warfare research. No matter what people may think, you know, that work really *is* defensive. We're not trying to engineer new plagues—we're trying to find defenses against the plagues that other people might be breeding...are breeding. Whoever starts the first plague war, it won't be the people who fund our research. We do have some very dangerous organisms here, but they're very secure. Your friend didn't even try to lay his hands on them. The material he wanted isn't dangerous at all—not in itself."

"An immunoserum," I said, remembering what the man called Fisher had said. "What's Diwaniya?"

"It's a city in Iraq," said Austerling, dryly. "Saddam Hussein had a top-security research unit of his own there, before the war. The allies' special forces went in to raid it, some time before the invasion. They seized all the paperwork on Saddam's biological warfare program. Official channels directed it here."

I frowned. "He said that he'd been in Iraq," I said, slowly. "He must have been with the raiders. But what did he come here for, if he'd already had access to all the paperwork?"

135

"He came for the antidote, you stupid idiot," said Austerling, grinding the words out with all the venom he could muster. "We were given something the Iraqis had developed. We were asked to find an immunoserum as quickly as we could, just in case the stuff was used. It wasn't—but we had the serum ready anyway. The reason it wasn't used was that Saddam didn't have an immunoserum himself. There's no point in launching a plague war, you see, if you can't protect your own troops. Even Saddam wasn't *that* crazy. I have no way of knowing how many people inside and outside Iraq have stockpiles of this particular bug, but until now none of them dared use it. I've no way of knowing, either, just what your friend is going to do with the antidote he took—but if I had to guess, I'd guess that he intends to do a little tiger-hunting with it. What do you think, Dr. Marlow?"

I saw, finally, what all Napier's talk about the necessity of control had been aiming at. Whatever faction he represented was anxious about the rapid progress made by humankind. They wanted to put a brake on. But mass murder isn't our style. To be that direct, we'd have to come out of hiding. *Our* style is more along the lines of 'let's you and him fight'. Napier's masters didn't want to launch a plague war themselves—they just wanted to make it easier for the humans to do it to one another...and, of course, to make absolutely sure that they themselves weren't caught in any crossfire.

"They're going to give it to Saddam," I whispered. "They're going to hand a super weapon to the craziest human on Earth—to a man who won't give a damn if millions of his own people perish with the enemy, as long as his inner circle is protected."

Austerling shrugged. "Maybe not to Saddam," he said. "There isn't any shortage of lunatics of his particular stripe. And you know who else won't give a damn, provided that they can protect themselves, don't you? There's *us*, of course—not just Napier's faction, but all the others too. They'll just shrug their shoulders and congratulate themselves on not having been forced to make the nasty decision. And do you think for a single minute that the human rulers of any Western country are going to shed too many tears over the depopulation of the Third World, or the Middle East, or even their own constituencies...just so long as they can protect themselves. Don't worry about it too much, Francis. If Napier hadn't done it, Kelly might have...and if not Kelly, Fisher...and if not Fisher...choose any name you want to, Francis. Any name at all."

I looked at him, dumbfounded.

"It was inevitable," he said, with a sigh. "It's been inevitable ever since they cracked the genetic code. We've already started talking about warfare in terms of biological analogies: surgical strikes, clinical bombing. What is war, at the end of the day, but a phase in the eternal Darwinian struggle of the genes...the competition between and within species? You and I know that better than anyone, don't we Francis? *We* understand. And we know, don't we, who the only *real* winners of the impending plague wars are going to be? After Armageddon, our kind will *really* be in control."

I looked away. I turned away from his sardonic smile, and I looked at Mary, who was lying in the bed with her eyes closed, slowly and peacefully reverting to her true, mock-human self.

She had a way to go yet, but she wasn't a monster any more.

I felt, just then, that the only monster in the room was me.

Austerling was right, of course. I could see that. It *was* inevitable—all of it. I had no need to feel unduly guilty because of the tiny part I'd played in oiling the wheels of change.

I glanced at the dead man, too. He was the most placid of us all—the only one who didn't have to cope with anxiety and guilt, loneliness and fear.

We all ride tigers, I thought. *Whatever and whoever we are, we all have our particular tigers to ride. And it doesn't really matter, when you get right down to basics, how good we are at keeping our particular secrets and serving our particular causes. When the ride ends, it's always the tiger that wears the smile.*

It was a bleak thought. It made me lean forward, and take my sister's shoulders in my arms. I drew her body towards me, and cradled her head upon my chest. Soon, she would be the Mary I knew and loved—the Mary I hadn't held in my arms for far too long.

Some day, I knew, our kind would be forced to own up to who and what we were. The mere appearance of humanity would not be sufficient to conceal our existence and our difference. Maybe, as Napier's faction obviously hoped, we could kill off enough humans before that day came to become the dominant species, and maybe that would be a reward of sorts for millions of years of patience and discretion. It wasn't what I wanted, and I didn't like being manipulated into serving that cause, but at the end of the day we all have to come to terms with who and what we are, and what we're prepared to do for the sake of those we love.

I hugged my sister, and hummed the tune of the oldest song I knew, and tried to remember the beautiful sound of her singing voice.

CURIOUSER AND CURIOUSER

A Kitchen Sink Drama

by Carol Lewis

Alice had just finished the washing-up. She was pouring the stained and greasy water out of the washing-up bowl when her wedding-ring slipped off her finger. The brown vortex carried it triumphantly away down the plug-hole. The sound of wild laughter echoed in the distance.

Alice didn't have time to think. Instinct took over, and before she could blink she was chasing after the ring. It wasn't until she came to an abrupt halt in the miry dark, landing on her a**e with a sticky splash, that she realized that she shouldn't have been able to fit down the plug-hole.

"I can't possibly be here," she said, aloud, while she wondered exactly where she was.

"According to Descartes," a deep and doleful voice replied, "the fact that you can think such a thought is adequate proof that you must be here. It's the fundamental existentialist conundrum that ties us all in knots."

"Who the h**l are you?" she asked.

There was a sudden flicker of light, and she saw a giant amoeba with glaring eyes and a vicious sneer holding a candle. "I'm a victim of false advertising," the amoeba said. "I used to look quite neat and trim in the days before Domestos commercials. Now I'm the next worst thing to Myra Hindley's mug shot. I'm the Unknown Germ—the one that strong bleach doesn't kill."

"Where am I?" Alice asked. "And how did I get here?"

"You're in the you-bend," the Unknown Germ told her. "You got here through the waist-disposal unit. It's better than any diet. The real question is: *why* are you here? I love existentialism, don't you?"

"I'm looking for my wedding-ring," Alice explained.

"Well, it's no wonder you're in the you-bend. Nothing gets a woman quite as bent out of shape as a wedding-ring, even though it's the existential conundrum that actually tightens the knot. You might as well give up. If it's gone down the drain, the Mad Housewife will have it by now. She *loves* wedding-rings. I keep telling her, a woman needs a man like a Cheshire Cat needs a grin, but will she listen?"

"Shouldn't that be *like a fish needs a bicycle*?" Alice asked.

"Down here," the Unknown Germ assured her, "every fish needs a bicycle. A coy carp wouldn't be seen dead without one."

"But surely Cheshire Cats need grins, too," Alice said. "Isn't the grin the very essence of a Cheshire Cat—the one thing that distinguishes it from all other cats?"

"All talk of essences is philosophically obsolete, in my opinion," the Unknown Germ informed her, loftily. "You might as well say that a wedding-ring is the very essence of a Mad Housewife—it doesn't *add* anything. Anyway, there's absolutely nothing to grin about down here. The Joker couldn't raise a smile at Batman's funeral."

"But I distinctly heard laughing as I fell into the plughole," Alice said.

"That was the hyenas. If you want to get straightened out, you know, you can't stay here. I'd go back if I were you. Except, of course, that I couldn't possibly be you, because if I were I wouldn't be me, so there wouldn't be any I to do the being—or if there were, there wouldn't be any you to do the being done, if you see what I mean."

Unfortunately, the candle went out while the sentence was still incomplete, so Alice couldn't see what he meant at all. It was a problem she'd often had with the males of her own species.

"I have to go on," she told the uncaring darkness. "I have to find my wedding-ring."

"There's nowhere to go but do-o-o-wn the dra-a-ain," the Unknown Germ's voice assured her, distorted by the Doppler effect as she was carried further on by a new tide of detergent-softened grease.

* * * * * * *

Eventually, Alice came to a rest again, floundering in gluey filth. By this time, she was so wound up that she had difficulty telling her a**e from her elbow. This time, there was natural light of a sort filtering through a grid high above her head so she could see something of her surroundings. She was in a deep hole, with no light at either end of the tunnel that stretched away—apparently to infinity—in front of her and b****d.

A coy carp cycled slowly past. It looked at her askance, but it didn't say anything. The bicycle's saddle looked profoundly uncomfortable, and Alice shuddered to think what a contraption of that kind might do to a cod's peace of mind on a long journey.

"There aren't any cod here, ducky," said a voice even more doleful than the Unknown Germ's, but not as deep. "Not enough salt. There wouldn't be any freshwater fish, either, if it weren't for the bicycles."

Alice peered into the gloomy covert to her left, and eventually managed to make out the face of the gloomiest she-cat she'd ever seen. The cat could have upstaged Elaine Page by the length of good-sized proscenium arch."

"You're the grinless Cheshire Cat, I assume," Alice said. "Re-emphasizing by your very existence the rule that everything down here is a**e-about-face."

"I used to be a Cheshire Cheese," the cat informed her, with the dubious dignity of the disabled, "before I was left in the fridge too long and went all furry. Once I was flush with youth, but I ended up being flushed. Don't we all?"

"Cheeses can't turn into cats," Alice objected. "The origin of species is a much slower process than that. I know my Darwin."

"The welsh rarebit you had for supper has already turned into you," the Grinless Cheshire Cat pointed out. "Mostly. Anyway, the real question is: do you know your darling. Or, more to the point, does your darling know you?"

Alice knew very well what the rest of the rarebit had turned into...but she didn't want to spell it out. Under other circumstances, she might have thought *Let's not go there*, but as she already was there, there didn't seem to be much point. As for her darling....

"I'm looking for the Mad Housewife," Alice said, figuring that she'd lose the last vestiges of dramatic tension if she let the plot stand still much longer. "According to the Unknown Germ, she probably has my wedding-ring."

"Almost certainly," the Grinless Cheshire Cat agreed. "Who else would want it?"

"Can you point me in the right direction?"

"Since you've been through the you-bend," the cat observed, "that would be exceedingly difficult. You'll have to get straightened out first. You'd better have a word with the Sewer Rats."

As the cat pronounced these last words the sound of hectic laughter rang out again, weirdly amplified by the infinite and strangely mazy conduits before and b****d.

"Is that the hyenas?" Alice wanted to know.

"Nothing else laughs down he-e-ere," the Grinless Cheshire Cat said, its voice distorted by the Doppler shift as it raced away into the deeper darkness.

Alice would have run too, had she not been swept away by a sudden deluge of soapy water cascading from the grid.

* * * * * * *

When she managed to get her head above water again Alice was surrounded by Sewer Rats. She knew what they were because they all had tape measures wound around their necks and needles of assorted sizes clutches in their paws. They all looked slightly nervous.

"It's okay," the smallest of them called to the others, "It's not the Unpied Piper. Poor thing looks as if she never had a pie in her life, although she's so wound up you'd need a pi to turn her diameter into a circumference. She must have gone through a waist-disposal unit and a you-bend."

"Isn't it the Pied Piper that's supposed to be dangerous?" Alice asked the smallest rat.

"He specializes in children nowadays," one of the larger rats told her. "It's just his evil twin that *we* have to look out for. He didn't want to be a thing of thread and patches any more, so we made him a beautiful suit—grey serge, it was. Unfortunately, he refused to pay us, so we had to send the Penalty Clause after him. That's Santa's evil twin, of course—best repo man in the Underworld. The Unpied Piper ended up stark naked and deep in the s**t. He's been looking to get his own back for years, but we sold the damn thing to John Major. No demand down here."

"I'm looking for the Mad Housewife," Alice said, deciding that it was time to move the plot forward again, "but the Cheshire Cat said that I needed to get straightened out first. She said that you might be able to help."

"Oo-oo-ooh," said the smallest Sewer Rat, totally unaided by the Doppler effect. "I don't know about that, love. We've got the needles all right—but can you pass through the eye of one?"

"I'm not trying get to Heaven," Alice assured the rats, "And I'm certainly not rich. Or a man. Or a camel." She was getting confused.

"You'd better be careful about mixing your metaphors down here, ducky," the oldest and dirtiest of the rats advised her, "or the hyenas will get you." Bang on cue, the sound of wild laughter echoed in the distance.

"Look," said Alice, "can you help me or not? I have to get on. Time's pressing."

"Time will only iron you flat," the smallest rat assured her. "To get properly straightened out, you need to get through *this*."

This was the eye of the thinnest of all the needles in the Sewer Rats' collection. Alice could see why the Sewer Rat didn't think she could get through it. It would have taken her quite some time just to thread it, even if she hadn't been mixing her drinks—or, come to that, her metaphors.

"She can do it," said another of the Sewer Rats. "There's hardly anything of her now she's been though the waist-disposal unit."

"Not all knotted up like that, she can't," opined another (it was a pity, Alice thought, that the Idle Author hadn't bothered to give the Sewer Rats names, although she didn't suppose that she'd be able to remember them all and she didn't expect to be meeting them again in a later chapter).

"She'll never get back into her wedding-ring, though," said yet another, "even if she can persuade the Mad House-wife to give it up."

"I suppose we'd better give it a try," the smallest rat said. "Not to do so would be to endorse, if only tacitly, the common human misconception regarding our essentially nasty nature."

The smallest Sewer Rat brought the needle down eye-first on Alice's head. His companion had been right about the knot causing trouble, but the smallest rat simply wouldn't give up, even though he wasn't cornered.

In the end, her skull changed shape to meet the aperture, and although there was a distinctly hairy moment when it reached her hips, the rat managed to pass it over her entire body from top to toe.

It was a little like trying to squeeze into a size ten in the M&S changing-room, but the ultimate result was a little more satisfactory.

Alice was about to say thanks when she realized that the Sewer Rats had fled in sudden panic.

She turned round, half-expecting to see the Unpied Piper in all his intimidating, deeply s**t-encrusted nakedness, but what she actually saw was much worse than that.

* * * * * * *

Alice woke up with a thundering headache to find herself spread-eagled in a pool of something unmentionable even with the aid of asterisks. She was staring into the bland blue eyes of a woman who might have been her twin sister, if she'd ever had a twin sister.

"What happened?" Alice asked.

"You got caught up by a Nasty Cliffhanger and fell into a text break," the woman told her, gloomily. "It happens."

Alice wasn't entirely sure that there weren't a couple of asterisks missing from that "it", but she decided that she was orally bound to give Idle Author the benefit of the d***t.

She rubbed her eyes, trying to make the headache go away. It wouldn't. When she stopped rubbing she took a longer look at her apparent twin. There had been too much talk of evil twins to allow her to look into a replica of her own face without trepidation, but she was reassured when she saw that the other woman wasn't *exactly* like her. The third finger on the other left hand was decked from root to fingernail with gold rings. There must have been at least a dozen.

"Thirteen actually," the Mad Housewife said, knowing what Alice was thinking because she was still keeping one eye on the unfolding narrative even though she should have been concentrating on her own lines now that she'd finally been shunted out of the wings to centre stage.

"That's an unlucky number," Alice pointed out. "Perhaps you'd better give mine back."

"On the contrary," The Mad Housewife said. "When it comes to wedding-rings, *one* is unlucky, *two* is the triumph of hope over experience and three is absolute b****y stupidity. Thirteen is so absurd as to be merely surreal. Anyway, now you've been through the waist disposal unit and the you-bend, and finally got yourself straightened out again, you don't need it any more. When that rarebit's fully digested you might even get your grin back—always assuming that it didn't pick up any Unknown Germs. Streptococcal diarrhea is *so* undignified."

"Oh f**k," Alice said. "I've just figured out what's happening here. That f****g cheese-on-toast is giving me f****g nightmares. I knew I shouldn't have exceeded the sell-by date. Can I wake up now?"

"Wake up!" screeched the Mad Housewife, laughing hysterically. "Wake up! You should be so lucky! Hey, you lot, listen to this. The silly cow only wants to wake up!"

"Wake up!" echoed the deep and doleful voice of the Unknown Germ, without the ghost of a Doppler shift.

"Doesn't she realize that it's me who's dreaming her? That's a laugh!" And he too joined in the chorus of laughter

"Wake up!" echoed the voice of the Grinless Cheshire Cat, s screechy as the plaint of a cod on a bicycle. "Nobody down here *ever* wakes up!" The quality of her caterwauling immediately revealed the reason why neither T. S. Eliot nor Andrew Lloyd-Webber had bothered to create a part for her.

"Wake up!" echoed the Sewer Rats, who sounded quite tuneful as an *ensemble* but had no chance at all of eclipsing the discordant voices of their companions. "Who does she think she is?"

"You're just a pack of hyenas!" Alice shouted. "I see it all now! You're just taking the p***!"

* * * * * * *

At this point, Alice suddenly realized, somewhat to her distress, that she wasn't dreaming at all. She was merely sitting in her kitchen, as neatly-clad as an Unpied Piper before a visit from the Penalty Clause, looking into a mirror and reflecting sadly on what she saw there. She hadn't been through the waist-disposal unit and you-bend at all, and she hadn't been straightened out either, worse luck. She still had her wedding-ring on her finger. Fortunately, she hadn't time for self-recriminations, with or without asterisks; the washing-up needed doing.

Time was pressing, and she wasn't completely ironed out yet.

Given time, though, she probably would be.

* * * * * * *

ABOUT THE AUTHOR

Between the ages of five and thirteen Carol Lewis *pursued a successful career as a nude model, but she never caught up with it. The experience proved the ideal preparation for marriage to a non-conformist minister. She is currently in the process of becoming divorced from reality, but reality has*

146

*not yet given up hope of achieving a reconciliation before
the granting of the decree absolute.*

QUALITY CONTROL

Brewer hadn't been in the Goat and Compasses for nearly a year. He didn't need to go into places like that nowadays; he always met his runners on safer ground. His legitimate business was booming and it didn't seem politic to be frequently seen in a pub known to be favored by dealers, pimps and other assorted riff-raff. There were no big players on view now, though; it was only lunchtime.

He found Simple Simon propping up the bar, looking no fatter and no more prosperous than he ever did, but not looking like a boy on the brink of starvation either. Brewer still thought of Simon as a boy although he must have been well into his twenties by now. Clearly, he was still working—if not for Brewer then for someone else.

"Hello, Simon," Brewer said, taking the youth by the elbow and leading him away from the bar to a booth in the corner. "It's been too long, hasn't it?" While Simon thought about how to answer that he went back to the bar and ordered a couple of pints.

When Brewer carried the tankards over to the booth and set them down Simon had the grace to look slightly guilty, but he didn't look scared. Brewer had never mastered the delicate art of terrifying his pushers, preferring to represent himself as a man who was as gentle and trustworthy as his product. Sometimes, he regretted his laxity. There was always the chance that some under-terrorized imbecile would grass him up if the police put the screws on tight enough.

"It's okay," he said, staying in character. "No threats. I only want an explanation. You owe me that much, at least."

"An explanation of what?" Simon asked, although he knew full well.

148

"An explanation of why you haven't picked up your supplies lately. I know you too well to believe that you've decided to straighten up, so you've obviously found an alternative supplier. You don't have to tell me who it is, but I need to know what it is you're peddling. I thought I had the kind of product that wouldn't easily be outdone. If my recipe book is out of date I really ought to catch up. It's not the money, of course—it's a matter of professional pride."

"It's not better," the youth muttered. "Not really. It's just different. New."

"You're telling me you're a fashion victim? Some new designer product hits the street and you feel like you have to switch brands in case your mates think your habit's passé?" Brewer tried hard to imply that it was unbelievable, but he knew that it was only too likely.

"It's not like that," Simon said, uncomfortably. "It's just...people can be very persuasive."

"You mean they threatened to break your legs if you didn't ditch my stuff and start selling theirs?"

"Not exactly," the boy muttered, unable to muster enough conviction to tell a convenient lie. The trouble with Simon was that he was vulnerable to the mildest forms of persuasion, provided he was approached in the right way.

"It's okay," Brewer lied, hoping that he didn't sound too convincing. "It was bound to happen. It's the hectic pace of technological innovation—not to mention the money that's being poured into neurochemical research. I'm only one man, and I can't be expected to create and supervise the psychotropic revolution by myself. There's room for everyone in a boom market, no need for conflict. This is 1999, after all—we're not Jurassic crack dealers, are we? I just need to know what's going on. Is there any reason why you shouldn't retail my products as well as theirs?"

Simon shrugged awkwardly. Plainly there was.

Brewer wondered whether it might have been optimistic to assume that his new rivals were men like him: civilized people with degrees, well-appointed laboratories, and a serious interest in the next phase of human evolution. Maybe the old-time crack dealers were trying to get back into the game. If so, he shuddered to think what their quality control must be like. He stared over Simon's shoulder and let his eyes wander while he wondered how much trouble he might be in.

His wandering gaze was suddenly arrested and held by a trim figure easing its way out of a booth on the far side of the room. His attention would have been caught even if he hadn't recognized the face lurking behind the opaque sunglasses, but the shock of realizing who she was intensified his reaction considerably.

Simon looked around to see what Brewer was staring at, but turned back quickly, as if he were afraid to look upon such a startling profile.

"Does she come in here often?" Brewer asked.

"Sometimes. Still counts a few of the working girls as friends. They say her old man doesn't like it, but he doesn't keep tabs on her during the day."

"Must be the laid-back type." Brewer used the sneer to cover up an unexpected stab of jealousy. For nearly a year Brewer had supplied Jenny with happy pills in exchange for sex, but she'd been using too many other things, and she'd never quite come off the game. He'd dumped her when she'd gone far enough downhill not to be special any more. In his experience, nobody ever climbed back up that kind of hill once they'd started to roll, but Jenny now looked extra special—far better than she ever had before. That was difficult to believe, given that she must be at least Simon's age, with the sweet succulence of innocence far behind her.

"So laid-back he's creepy," Simon said. "You want to go say hello?" He didn't really think he was going to be let off that easily, but there was a distinct note of hope in his voice, doubtless encouraged by the intensity of Brewer's stare. He wouldn't have got off that easily, either, if the girl hadn't got up from her seat at that very moment and started for the door, waving goodbye to her erstwhile friends—who looked after her with naked envy, but rather less hatred than might have been expected.

Brewer didn't spare Simon another glance, but he said "I'll be back" in his best Schwarzenegger drawl. He left the pint he'd hardly touched on the table.

* * * * * * *

It wasn't difficult to catch up with Jenny; she wasn't hurrying.

"Can I offer you a lift somewhere," Brewer said, as he drew level with her.

She seemed genuinely surprised to see him. Perhaps she'd been too deep in conversation to see him enter the pub and perhaps she hadn't glanced in his direction while she made for the door. She stopped and turned to look up into his eyes. Her own eyes were hidden by the dark glasses but he imagined them blue and clear, as radiant as her complexion.

"I don't know, Bru," she said, blithely. "Which way are you going?"

"Any way you like," he said. "It's my afternoon off."

"Nothing cooking back at the lab?" Her voice was gently teasing; there was no evidence of hard feelings regarding the way their previous acquaintance had drifted to its end.

"We only do the lawful stuff by day," he told her. "Half the night too, most days. Difficult to find time for fun and games. The last civil service lab's due to close next April—not cost effective. Private contractors like me do all the statutory health and safety work these days, as well as all the forensic testing. Never been busier."

"Health and safety work? Is that what you call it?"

It was more a veiled insult than a joke. He'd always offered products that were as safe and as healthy as he could contrive. He liked all his customers to stay fit and well—and happy too.

"Quality control is what I call it," he said. "Making sure that the goods you buy at the supermarket, or over the pharmacist's counter, are exactly what they're supposed to be and as pure as scientific ingenuity can make them. It's vital work in these corrupt times. There's more money in faking designer drugs than there is in faking designer jeans or fine wines, and you know how paranoid people are about their food since last year's pesticide plague. You look incredibly well, Jenny. I'd never have believed it. You must have kicked all your old habits." He emphasized the word *all* very slightly.

"Every last one," she said. "Where's your car."

"In the multi-storey. I never park illegally. Where do you want to go? Home?" He started walking again as he said it, pointing the way with a languid finger

"I guess." She must have known that he was burning with curiosity, but she carefully didn't say where home was. "Everything's rosy with you, then?"

"Couldn't be better," he assured her, having no intention of telling her that some rival was taking a big bite out of his synthetics trade. "The revolution is bang on course. The great crusade continues." He always took care to sound as if he wasn't serious when he said things like that, but he was. He didn't see himself as one more drug-peddler in the shark-infested soup; he really did believe that psychotropic chemistry would pave the way for the next step in human evolution. He'd tried to explain that to Jenny a dozen times and more, back in the old days.

"I know," she said, perhaps implying that, although she'd kicked the habits that had been destroying her, she hadn't given up on everything she bought on the street...or perhaps not.

"I hear you're living with a laid-back creep," he said, as they stepped into the lift that would take them up to level nine of the multi-storey. "Only comes out at night—some kind of vampire, maybe?"

She didn't laugh. She didn't even smile. In fact, she turned her head away, as if she didn't want him to be able to read her reaction too accurately. As she moved her head the skin at the side of her neck stretched, and lifted an odd discoloration briefly into view above the collar of her neat black blouse. It looked like a love bite, but Brewer only caught a momentary glimpse of it before she turned again and it disappeared.

"I'm with someone," she admitted. "I'm not like I used to be, Bru. I learned to apply a little quality control of my own, just in time."

This time the insult wasn't even veiled.

"It's okay," Brewer said, uneasily. "I'm only curious, not jealous. We were never married, were we?"

"No," she said, colorlessly. "We never were."

152

When she got into the car—without pausing to admire it, although it certainly warranted a certain respect—she had to tell him where home was.

"Docklands?" he echoed, deliberately overdoing the contempt. "I thought even the yuppie dinosaurs had moved out of there. I suppose it's handy for your old stamping grounds, though."

"It's quiet," she said, as if that were explanation enough. Then she looked away, as if she wanted to punish him for wanting to hurt her feelings—but she didn't try to get out of the car again, and she seemed perfectly relaxed as he zig-zagged down to the barrier and out into the traffic.

He let the conversation lapse while he threaded his way through the crowded streets, pretending to concentrate hard but continually stealing sidelong glances at her at every junction. She gave him directions in an absurdly overabundant fashion, as if he couldn't be trusted to find his way around the City Security Zone or through the road-works fringing the last of the Jubilee Line extension building-sites.

* * * * * * *

The place to which Jenny eventually guided him was, indeed quiet—which wasn't surprising, given that it was one of those maximum security buildings with a fiendishly complicated entry system and no ground floor windows.

"Are you going to invite me in for a coffee?" he asked, as she got out. She hesitated, with her hand on the door-handle, as if waiting for some extra inducement. Thinking that he understood, he reached under the seat and released his secret stash. "I can sweeten it for us," he said.

"You're crazy, keeping that stuff in your car," she said. "Especially a thief-magnet like this."

"We scientific geniuses have ways of thief-proofing our homes and vehicles," he said, airily. "We don't need that kind of hi-tech fortress." He nodded at the armored entry-door with all its smart sensors.

She let go of the door-handle without opening the door. "If you're coming up for coffee," she said, "you'd better put the car in the basement. And if you want it sweet, you can

153

have all the sugar you need. Put that stuff back where it came from."

He did as he was told. It would have suited him better if she'd been tempted, but he certainly wasn't going to insist.

It was almost as difficult to get into the subterranean car park as it was to get through the building's main door, and Jenny had to produce two different ID cards to open the doors of the lift which took them up to the apartments—all the way up, as it transpired. Jenny's new man lived in the penthouse.

"The trouble with security," Brewer observed, as they made their ascent, "is that it works both ways. If there were a fire, you'd never get out—and the fire brigade wouldn't be able to get in to help you. Where I live, it's simple to get in and out, even though it's not easy. My security systems are glorious in their subtlety."

"Just like you," she said, with telling sarcasm. Perhaps, he thought, she'd only invited him in to score a few points by showing him everything that she'd accomplished since he dumped her. On the other hand, living in a maximum-security love-nest with a guy that Simple Simon called a creep must have its downside. If she often went back to the Goat and Compasses, to pass the time of day with whores whose beat she'd once shared, she must be desperate for congenial company.

Brewer wasn't surprised to find that Jenny's boyfriend wasn't home. He was, however, mildly surprised to discover what kind of place his home was. It wasn't particularly plush, considering the rent one had to pay for that kind of situation and that kind of safety, and it was certainly no left-over yuppie's style-trap. All the walls were lined with shelves and all the shelves were fully-laden, ninety per cent with books and ten per cent with CDs: thousands of each. There was an alcove in the living-room fitted out as a work-station with a pair of widescreen PCs whose screen savers swirled different shades of blue and grey around one another in endless mirror-image sequences. Brewer took note of the laser-printer and the idle fax machine, but they weren't interesting enough to warrant close study. The glass in the broad window was heavily smoked; even though the sun was shining, the room was distinctly dim.

It would have taken hours to make a detailed study of all the book-titles, but a quick scan told him that they were all non-fiction, with no obvious specialism. The CDs were mostly audio or read-only, but there were at least fifty user-discs. If they weren't just for show, that added up to an awful lot of gigabytes.

"Are you taking an Open University degree or something?" he asked, although he was painfully aware that it left much to be desired as a conversational gambit."

"No," she said, disappearing into the kitchen to put the kettle on. She had finally taken off her sunglasses, but he still hadn't seen her eyes.

"Mind if I use your loo?" he asked, figuring that he would only get eaten away by curiosity if he didn't."

"Into the hallway, second door on the right," she answered, unsuspiciously.

The bathroom was ordinary enough. He turned the taps on while he opened the cabinet and began a scrupulous examination of everything stored there. His trained eye skated over the cosmetics and probed for something that didn't look quite right, something revealing. He didn't expect any illegals, or even anything particularly esoteric, but in his experience there were always clues in a bathroom cabinet for an expert eye to decode.

He grinned when he found three pill-bottles without proprietory or prescription labels lurking in a corner behind a flask of skin-conditioner. When he shook the capsules out he saw that they didn't have any indicative markings. He picked up three of each kind of capsule, slipped them into the inside pocket of his jacket and turned the taps off.

By the time he came out he'd triggered Jenny's urge to go. When she locked the door behind her he moved swiftly into the kitchen and opened the refrigerator, just on the off chance.

This time the anomaly leapt right out at him. Three non-standard hooks had been installed in the left-hand wall and the grille below them had had two bars removed so that three fluid-filled bags could be hung there. Brewer didn't like to judge by appearances, but the straw-colored fluid that filled the bags looked like blood-plasma—the real thing, not the standard synthetic substitute. He just had time to squeeze a sample into one of the specimen-bottles he always carried with him before moving swiftly back to the living-room and taking up his coffee-cup.

"Well," he said to Jenny, as she came back into the room "you certainly landed on your feet. I'm glad. How did you kick the hard stuff—some kind of substitution program?" Her eyes were blue and radiant, exactly as he'd expected, and they had a curious haunted look that was very attractive—as if they had seen far more than they had ever hoped or expected to.

"Will power," she said, shortly. "You don't seem too have taken too much harm from sampling your own products—but you were always a moderate man. I suppose you've got plenty of girlfriends, just as lovely and every bit as eager as I was?"

"No one special," he said.

"No one is," she retorted. He wondered if it was a philosophical remark or yet another insult, to be understood as including an unspoken *to you*.

"Anyhow," he told her, truthfully, "I don't know anyone as lovely as you. You used to be pretty, all right, but now...what's your secret, Jenny? I bet those kids you were talking to in the pub would give a hell of a lot to know it." He couldn't help adding: "They must really hate you now."

"It's no secret, Bru," she said. "It was just a matter of getting the shit out of my system. I'm okay now—absolutely clean. Nobody hates me. I don't go back there to rub their noses in it. They know I only want to help."

Saint Jennifer, reformed whore and would-be savior of fallen women? he was tempted to say. All he actually said was: "Nobody's absolutely clean." He held up the coffee-cup as he said it, to remind her that caffeine was an upper of sorts. The coffee was too strong for his taste, and he noticed that she was drinking hers black, without sweeteners. She'd always liked it white before, with one or even two.

She didn't dignify his stupid correction with a reply.

"The light in here is distinctly dismal," Brewer observed, feeling that he'd somehow gone five points down in the game and hadn't a clue how to start scoring on his own account. "I don't wonder you feel the need to get out in the sun once in a while, even if you have to go back to your old haunts in search of a bit of company. Don't you have new friends now? Or is your boyfriend the solitary type, outside of bed?"

"You'd probably get on with him well enough," Jenny told him, wryly. "You have lots of interests in common."

Brewer let his eyes travel over the loaded bookshelves. "He probably has interests in common with everyone who has interests," he remarked. "He's obviously a very interested man. Is that why you're at a loose end? Is he out pursuing his interests?"

"He doesn't have a lot of free time at the moment."

"I know the feeling," Brewer said. "Exactly what interests do he and I have in common?"

"Biotech," she said, shortly. After a pause, she added: "Quality control." Now she was being deliberately enigmatic. Her blue eyes were looking up at him from beneath slightly lowered brows. She was fishing for a reaction. Brewer wondered whether she expected him to be flattered by the news that she'd picked out a man like himself once she'd been consumed by conformity and decency—if she had been consumed by decency and conformity, and wasn't just a better class of whore than she'd been before.

"Are you happy?" he asked.

"What kind of question is that?"

"Just a question."

"Do you think I was happy before?" she asked, with some slight asperity. "Do you think I was happy when I knew you?"

"You were sometimes," he said. "I was the one who gave you the happy pills, remember. I make a good product. You were happy enough when you were under the influence. I just wondered if you were happy now that you don't even take sweeteners in your caffeine-loaded coffee."

"What you're wondering," she said, "is why I invited you up here, and why I agreed to let you drive me home.

You're wondering whether you might possibly have got lucky, now that screwing me would count as *getting lucky* instead of trivial commerce."

"I never thought of it like that," Brewer said, as equably as he could.

"No, you didn't. For me, trading sex for the stuff you had to sell was cutting out the middleman, but you really did think that it didn't count as whoring if no actual money changed hands. I never quite understood that."

"I liked you," he said, truthfully. "You were pretty, and sweet. Are you pissed because I never asked you to let me take you away from all the rest of it? I might have, if I'd thought you'd say yes—but you were the one who was just cutting out the middleman."

"I'm a lot prettier now," she said, "but not nearly so sweet. I'm not so sure you'd like me now, once you got to know me." The haunted note was sounding in her voice now.

"I'm sure," Brewer told her. He intended it as a compliment, but she didn't seem to take it that way.

"Because nothing else counts except the looks," she countered. "Because getting to know me better couldn't possibly change your mind, which you made up the instant you saw me in the Goat and Compasses. What were you doing there, anyway? I haven't seen you in there before—not for at least a year."

"Looking up an old friend," he told her. "You remember Simon, don't you? Simple Simon."

"Oh, him," she said, as if the revelation explained everything.

"He's no worse than the old friends you were looking up," Brewer pointed out. "Maybe a cut above, depending how you compare things. Either way, he brought us together again. It really is good to see you, and I really am pleased that you got out of the gutter and started reaching for the stars. Sure you're happy. Who wouldn't be? So why did you let me drive you home instead of calling me a shit and kicking me in the balls? If I was just a paying customer before, why give me the time of day now? If you don't want to pick up where we left off—and I assume you don't—you must have some little itch of curiosity needling you. You must at least be interested to know how I am."

"I already asked you how you were," she pointed out.

"So what else do you want to know?"

"How you really are. As you say, there's just a slight itch of nostalgic curiosity. Do you know the one thing about you I missed, when you stopped coming round because I was too much of a wreck?"

It wouldn't have been diplomatic to say *the pills* so Brewer said: "My acid wit?"

"Those little rhapsodies about the psychotropic revolution," she said. "Not the acidly witty ones, the ones when you forgot yourself just a little, and actually half-meant what you were saying, about a world where biotechnology would save us from ourselves. It was all bullshit, of course, but it was nice that you believed in something, even if it wasn't love or honesty or common decency. I was young then, of course. Too young. Do you still believe in it, just a little, or have you become just one more drug-peddler, dedicated to being rich and having a flash car with cunning anti-theft devices?"

"Oh, I still believe in it," Brewer assured her. "I really and sincerely do. I only use the acid wit to cover up that fact. Always speak the truth in a sarcastic tone of voice, and no one will ever find you out."

"No one?"

"Except you, of course. I let my guard down with you. I'm letting my guard down now, or hadn't you noticed? It came crashing down the moment I saw you in the pub. I should be busy breaking Simple Simon's legs, or persuading him that I might if he doesn't shape up, but I never had the heart for that kind of crap, and the moment I saw you...well, here we are. This is a terrible cup of coffee. How can you drink it black like that?" He put the cup down and moved closer to her, pretending that he was just pointing at her coffee cup.

"Our tastes change as we mature," she told him. She must have known that he wasn't moving closer to point to her coffee cup, but just for a moment she hesitated about backing away. He took that as a green light, but when he reached out for her she froze. He'd gone too fast.

"No, Bru," she said. "It's nothing like that. It really was just curiosity."

He didn't believe her. He took hold of her anyway, hoping that it might be the kind of stall that could still be over-ridden, although he knew that the odds were against him, for the time being. He tried to kiss her, but she wouldn't be kissed. He held her more firmly, but when she stopped struggling it wasn't surrender.

"You'd have to rape me," she said. "I don't think you want to do that, do you?"

He let go of her immediately. It certainly wasn't what he wanted, and it definitely wasn't his style.

"There's nothing I have to offer you any more, I suppose?" he said, not intending it to sound as bitchy as it did. "Nothing you want in return?"

She didn't look angry, but she didn't look apologetic either. "This was a mistake," she said. "It was silly."

"Not that silly," he assured her. "Whatever you were looking for back there, you were more likely to find in me than in those tattered slags you were talking to. You still are. What were you looking for? Not just something to relieve the boredom, surely."

"No," she said, positively. "Not just that. And you're right—maybe I should have come looking for you in the first place. But it's nothing to do with sex, Bru, nor with the stuff you peddle as synthetic happiness. It's something else. You'd better go now."

"Why?" he riposted. "Is it time for your boyfriend to come out of his coffin? Oh, sorry—home from work, I mean. What exactly is it that he does?" He was almost tempted to make a crack about the plasma in the fridge, but he knew better. One of his golden rules was never to tell people he knew they had secrets until he'd figured out what the secrets were.

"I wouldn't like to keep you away from your own work for too long," she countered. "All those hemorrhoid creams and heartburn tablets have to be kept pure, don't they? And there's always more happiness to cook up while the plant's lying idle. You always were a busy man—that's why your sex life consisted of brief encounters with cheap whores."

The insults were too far out of date to hurt. The new generation of pharmaceuticals was way past the hemorrhoid and heartburn phase.

"I knew the acid wit was what you'd missed most," he came back, as heroically as he could. "You obviously missed it so much you stole the recipe."

He left after that—as politely as he could, given the circumstances.

It wasn't easy to get the car out of the basement, but he managed it eventually. He drove it home, possessed all the while by an icy calm.

He was sure that he'd see her again, even though he'd made such an unholy mess of things. He'd memorized the number inscribed on the phone in her hallway, and he knew she'd probably be on her own during working hours. Next time, he'd have a script ready, and he'd make up all the ground he'd lost.

He had to; it was a matter of pride.

* * * * * * *

Brewer made no attempt to put the pills or the plasma into analysis while his lab-assistants were still on site. Even Johanna wouldn't have known what he was doing, or why, and she knew better than to ask, but it was his habit to be discreet and he needed the equipment in the main lab to get the job done quickly. Johanna and Leroy weren't in the least surprised that he was still there when they completed the last of their own assignments a mere two hours into time-and-a-half and dropped the results on his desk. They thought of him, half-admiringly and half-pityingly, as a workaholic night-bird.

He bid them both a cheery goodbye, and switched on all the privacy screens as soon as they were clear of the building.

Once he'd got the first set of analyses started, his curiosity faded away into the methodical routines. It wasn't until he was certain that it was a *very* exotic protein that a certain excitement began to force its way through his controlled state of mind. All proteins in the public domain were intrinsically boring; these days, one had to go a long way out of that domain to find anything really weird. This one was from way back in the wilderness.

When the first sample had cleared the first stage of analysis he set the replicated samples of the second compound going, but he held off on the plasma lest he get into a tangle. The first rule of good lab practice was to take things in order.

As soon as Brewer had an amino-acid map of the first compound, and while he was still waiting for its 3-D configuration, he checked the newest edition of the encyclopedia. He knew that the unknown wouldn't be on file—these days, nobody ever filed anything until they were sure it was worthless, and that usually took a long time—but he expected the book to throw up a few probable template-molecules based on common base-clusters. Practically all novel proteins were designed by computer programs that tried to juggle known activity-sites into more interesting or more economical configurations, so it was usually possible to guess what kind of base an innovation had started from and what kind of effect the designer might be trying to enhance.

It didn't take him long to figure out that he wasn't dealing with any of his usual fields. Whatever pill number one was supposed to do, it hadn't any obvious potential to mimic or interact with neurotransmitters or amygdalar encephalins. Nor had it any detectable kinship with the currently-favored avenues of research into cell-repair and tissue-rejuvenation. That probably meant that it had nothing to do with Jenny's new look—but if it had, then it really must be something odd, something unexpected.

It didn't take long to find out that the same was true of type two—by which time Brewer's instincts were beginning to detect a suspiciously natural ambience.

Brewer was not at all enthused by the thought that the samples might be nothing more than lumps of raw-material, churned out by DNA of unknown function that had been cloned from some obscure plant or bacterium in the faint hope that it might turn out to be interesting. Computerized design hadn't quite driven the old pick-and-mix methods to extinction and there wasn't a nation in the world that didn't have its own mock-patriotic Ark project dedicated to gene-banking as many local species as could be identified, in the faint hope of preserving data that would otherwise be lost to the attrition of routine extinction.

The trouble with natural proteins, of course, was that they might be geared to functions that had no relevance at all to human beings, slotted into biochemical systems that had long been discarded by the higher animals—or, indeed, all animals of whatever height. The majority of exotic natural proteins sufficiently stable to be incorporated into pills were structural materials devoid of any real physiological significance. Brewer tried to console himself with the thought that nobody would keep those kinds of samples in his bathroom cabinet, but it wasn't until he had the 3-D configurations, and could trace the pattern of active sites, that he became morally certain that he wasn't dealing with any mere building-blocks for fibers or cell-walls.

Unfortunately, it still wasn't clear exactly what the relevant physiological activity might be. The proteins certainly weren't psychotropics, and if they were cosmetics of some kind they were no common-or-garden patent-avoiders.

By the time he decided that it was time he put the plasma-like stuff into the system, he had been studying his screen intently for at least twenty minutes, virtually oblivious to his surroundings. While he reached out to pick up the specimen-bottle containing the straw-colored liquid his eyes still lingered on the screen. It wasn't until his groping hand failed to make contact with the bottle that he looked sideways, and then up.

There was no way to tell how long the invader had been standing there, not six feet away, watching him. Brewer had never been so startled in all his life—but he had never before been confronted by anything so nearly impossible. His electronic defenses were, as he had assured Jenny, glorious in their subtlety. How glorious, therefore, must be the subtlety of the man who now stood before him, having hacked his way through the undergrowth of passwords and booby-traps?

There was nothing particularly striking about the invader himself, apart from his lustrously pale skin, his remarkably dark eyes, and his astonishing aptitude for silence. He didn't seem unusually menacing, although there was a peculiar glint in his near-black eyes, which suggested that he might become menacing if crossed.

Brewer desperately wanted to say something that would save a little face, but he just wasn't up to it. All he said, in the end, was: "Who the hell are you?" He was uncomfortably aware of the fact that it was a very tired cliché.

"You've seen me before, Mr. Brewer," the unwelcome visitor told him. "Several times, in fact." He had a slight accent of some kind but it wasn't readily identifiable.

Brewer stared hard at the invader's face, certain that he would have remembered those coal-black eyes and that remarkable complexion. He had method enough left in him to realize that, if that were so, those were exactly the features he must set aside, in order to concentrate on the rest. When he did that, he got a dim impression of *where* he had seen the man—but, not, alas, the least flicker of a name.

On the other hand, Brewer realized, given what he was doing and the way his uninvited guest had taken the trouble to sit round and wait for him to look up, there couldn't be much doubt about the invader's purpose in coming to call.

"Jenny said we had interests in common," he said, knowing that there was far too much lost ground to catch up but feeling that he had to try. "You see so many people, though—all those seminars, all those cunningly-contrived meetings in which clients try to whip up competition in order to drive the tenders down. We were never formally introduced, were we? Funny how we can have so many mutual acquaintances, and not know one another at all."

"I know *you* very well," the stranger said. "I've heard a great deal about you, one way and another." There was suddenly something about his eyes that seemed profoundly unsettling, but there was as much sadness in it as threat.

Brewer, desperate to know exactly how much trouble he was in, tried to fathom the significance of *one way and another*. One way was obviously Jenny—but who was the other? The people Brewer met at conferences and the people he met in the course of his legitimate business had little or nothing to tell. He put two and two together and hoped he wasn't making five.

"You're the guy who's been taking over my runners, aren't you?" Brewer said, "Jenny put you on to them—to Simon and the others. Is that what she was doing in the Goat and Compasses today? Making deliveries?"

The stranger shook his head. "She doesn't make deliveries," he said. "She has nothing to do with that aspect of the business at all—except, of course, that she did give me the information that allowed me to make contact with some of your agents. I only needed a handful of names; the rest I did myself."

"Did she tell you where to find me?" Brewer asked, warily. He wondered whether the accent might be German, or maybe Serbian.

The stranger shook his head. "That was Simon," he said. "You embarrassed him. He told me you were after me—and why you suddenly stopped asking questions. Jenny doesn't know that I know you were at the flat, any more than she knows about the things you took. It was careless of me to leave them lying around, but I simply didn't realize that you might be able to walk through my security systems as easily as I could walk through yours."

That was a scoring point; without Jenny's help, Brewer would never have been able to worm his way into the stranger's flat, and they both knew it.

"Fate seems to have been determined to throw us together," Brewer observed. "Did you pick up my ex-girlfriend solely in order to find out about my distribution-system, or did she just happen to give you the idea of making a little extra money that way?"

"What do you make of the proteins?" the other asked, pointedly ignoring the question. "How much have you figured out?"

What Brewer had figured out was that the one advantage left to him might well be that the other man couldn't possibly know how little he knew, so he wasn't about to tell him.

"Jenny's looking very well," Brewer commented, instead. "Rather better than you are, I think—which presumably means that you're testing your freshly-hatched miracles on her before applying them to yourself. Sensible enough, I suppose, but not entirely sporting. No wonder Simon thinks you're a creep. You'll want to do a few more runs before you're certain, of course. Better safe than sorry." That was the best he could do without admitting that he hadn't a clue what the proteins were for, or where they might have come from.

"We're not enemies, Mr. Brewer," said the man with the disturbing eyes. "We're not even rivals—not really."

Brewer didn't understand that move either. Was the stranger trying to make a deal? If so, he thought, the best thing to do was play along with it. "Sure," he replied. "We're both on the same side: the side of the psychotropic revolution. We're marked down by destiny to be the midwives of the *übermensch*."

"Jenny told me all about that," the stranger admitted. "She told me that you were sincere, but I wasn't convinced."

"Is that why you're here—to be convinced?" Brewer couldn't believe it was as simple as that.

"Not exactly," said the dark-eyed man. "I came out of curiosity. While I'm here, though, I suppose I ought to recover the things you stole, and obliterate all the records of your analyses." He stressed the word *all* very faintly, perhaps to remind Brewer that memories were records too.

"I can understand that," Brewer said. "I'm irredeemably curious myself."

The stranger hesitated, as if he were hovering on the brink of some make-or-break decision. Then, making up his mind, he set the specimen-bottle down on the bench beside him and took something out of his pocket.

Brewer recognized the device immediately. It was a sterile pack containing a disposable drug-delivery device: what the tabloids had taken to calling a "smart syringe" since it had become the darling of all the hardcore mainliners. The instrument wasn't so very smart, but it was subtle; its bioconductors could deliver drugs to underlying tissues without ripping up the superficial tissues. Deeper probes did tend to break a few capillaries, but they only left a little round mark like a bruise—or a love bite.

166

"Need a fix?" Brewer asked, uneasily.

With a dexterity that might have been admirable in other circumstances the stranger took the cap off the specimen bottle one-handed and carefully transferred the fluid to the barrel of the device.

"Keep your hands on the bench," the stranger instructed him.

Brewer instantly raised his hands from the bench and came to his feet. He wasn't being stubborn or heroic—it was just a reflex, animated by fear. He swung his fist, the way he'd seen a hundred actors swing theirs in a hundred action-movies.

The dark-eyed man pivoted on his heel, and moved so fast that Brewer couldn't keep track of him. It might have been the blindness of Brewer's panic, but the speed of the man seemed supernatural. Brewer found himself reeling backwards, clutching his stomach. It hurt horribly, but he hadn't yet had the wind knocked out of him and he was able to lunge forward again, as if to tackle the other round the knees.

The second assault was no more effective than the first. The unseen blow to his head hurt even worse than the smack in the belly. It didn't leave Brewer unconscious, but it knocked him down and it knocked him silly. He was on all fours, wondering whether he could get up again, when he felt a foot in the small of his back, forcing him further down. He pressed upwards against the force, but he couldn't resist it. Once he was flat on the ground, with an irresistible weight bearing down on him, he felt the pressure-pad of the smart syringe at his neck.

The contact lasted at least twenty seconds, but there was nothing Brewer could do to break it. It didn't hurt—that, after all, was the whole point of smart syringes.

Brewer was slightly surprised that he was still conscious when the instrument as withdrawn, although there was no earthly reason to suppose that the straw-colored liquid might have been an anesthetic. By the time the weight was removed from his back the pain in his head was easily bearable, but he still felt nauseous. He thought it best to stay down until he was sure he could stand up straight. He was dimly conscious of the dark-eyed man moving to the bench where the pills were.

Eventually, he picked himself up, and met the stare of those remarkable eyes. "Thanks," he said, putting on the bravest face he could. "I thought I'd lost my chance to analyze the stuff."

"You've got every chance," the dark-eyed man assured him. "But there really isn't any hurry. Not now. You know where to find me when you're fully prepared for a rational discussion."

Having said that, the stranger simply turned away, walked to the door of the lab, and went out. It shouldn't have been easy to exit the building without the proper codes, but Brewer didn't suppose the unwelcome visitor would get into any difficulties.

A quick check told him that the remaining pills were gone and that the data displayed on his screen had all been dumped. It wasn't a thorough job, though; he probably had enough traces left in the equipment to do another run, and he ought to be able to recover the ghosted data from the hard disk. The dark-eyed man didn't seem to care what Brewer had found out, or what he still might find out. Brewer wondered exactly what the mysterious stranger had meant by "fully prepared". It couldn't be a simple matter of attitude.

Brewer used an ordinary hypodermic to extract some blood from the discolored patch at the side of his neck, but he didn't start any kind of immediate analysis; he stuck it in the refrigerator and hurried out into the night. He didn't stop until he reached a payphone.

He used a generic phone card of the kind anyone could buy at the checkout in any supermarket but he was careful to route the call through Talinn; the people whose help he needed preferred to deal with careful customers.

* * * * * * *

It was so late by the time Brewer got back on the road that Simple Simon was at home, sleeping the sleep of the unintimidated. Unsurprisingly, he was alone. His door had three good locks on it and his window had two, but the glass was so old it hadn't been proofed against solvents, so Brewer was able to get in without disturbing his host and conduct a rapid but thorough search.

He found Simon's supply easily enough, buried beneath the youth's collection of business cards. It was a collection like any other; Simon stripped telephone booths the way younger kids stripped foreign stamps from used envelopes. Brewer pocketed all but a few of the pills. Then he positioned himself by the side of Simon's bed.

He filled a common-or-garden hypodermic syringe that he hadn't bothered to sterilize, and pressed it suggestively to Simon's throat while switching on the bedside lamp. He wished that he'd made more effort to cultivate the expertise of intimidation. No matter how hard one tried to be business-like, it seemed, there was something about the drug business that resisted rational reform.

"Don't jump, Simon," he advised, as the boy's eyes flew open. "Quite apart from the fact that you'd impale your Adam's apple, you'd get a shot of something very nasty indeed."

Simon spluttered and twitched a bit, but he got the message.

"What is this?" he complained.

"Tell me about Jenny's boyfriend, Simon," Brewer said. "Tell me everything you know, and tell it fast."

"What's in the syringe?" Simon wanted to know.

"Just something to set your nerves jangling. It won't do any permanent damage, but it'll make every kind of sensory experience excruciatingly painful for at least twenty-four hours. If you don't want to live through the most godawful day imaginable, tell me about the guy who's fitting you out with your new supplies. Tell me everything, and pray that it might be enough."

Simon had been about to protest that he didn't know anything at all but he changed his mind. "He's a chemist, just like you," he said, as if that might make the news more welcome. "Analyses stuff for the government, or anybody else who pays...he says his name's Anthony Marklow, but I don't think he's even English. His stuff's not *better*, just different. I'm not about to stop using yours, believe me. It's just...."

"Marklow, Simon. Tell me about Marklow. What's Jenny been doing for him? Is she selling stuff to the whores—or giving it away? What is it?"

"I don't know! What's the matter with you? What was all that stuff about not being a gangster, hey? What was all that stuff about *room for everybody in a boom market?*"

"This isn't about economic competition, Simon. It's about something more serious. Marklow's not just hawking happy pills. He's doing something else, and I need to know what it is. *Now*, Simon. What's he doing as well as cutting into my trade?"

"How the fuck should I know?" the youth wailed, with patent sincerity. "I just...you'll have to ask the girls. Jenny talks to the girls, not to me. If she gives them something, they sure as hell don't tell me."

With the forefinger of his free hand Brewer pulled his collar down and pointed to the side of his neck, where there was a blue mark that would soon turn purple, and then brown. Simon's frightened eyes followed the gesture with mesmeric concentration.

"Have you seen anyone sporting marks like this?" Brewer asked.

"Sure," Simon told him. "I thought it was funny—the doc doesn't usually shoot stuff into a person's neck, and you wouldn't think the girls would do it to themselves. Why...?" He stopped, evidently wondering how the mark on Brewer's neck had got there but not daring to ask.

"How many?" Brewer wanted to know.

"I've seen three," Simon said, implying that there might be dozens or hundreds more. "Why the neck?"

"Maybe he doesn't have time to get them to roll their sleeves up," Brewer replied, drawing the point of the syringe an inch or two away from Simon's throat. A more likely explanation was that the target was the carotid artery, which would feed the drug straight into the brain—except that his brain still seemed to be working normally. He wasn't high and he wasn't dopey; whatever had been shot into his flesh hadn't been a psychotropic. Maybe the hit had been aimed at one of the brain's associated bodies. If so, the pituitary had to be the favorite, with the pineal close behind. The pituitary was the master gland, the dispatcher controlling the hormonal couriers which kept the body in order. The pineal still carried an aura of Cartesian mystery that had intrigued a legion of modern investigators.

Simon freed one of his naked arms from the duvet and reached out to push Brewer's hypodermic even further away. Brewer let him do it; if the boy had known anything more about Marklow he'd have spilled it.

"How long has Jenny looked the way she does now?" Brewer asked.

"Don't know," Simon replied, yet again. "She started coming around three, maybe four months ago. Every three weeks or so. Like I say, she doesn't talk to me. Just to the girls. I didn't know she was with the creepy guy, at first. I saw him pick her up one night. I've seen them together a couple of times since, always after dark. I thought...." He trailed off, as if no longer certain of what he had thought.

"Why *creepy*, Simon? What's so creepy about him?" Brewer realized as he posed the question that it might be important. "Creepy" wasn't the kind of word people like Simon usually bandied about; it was a whole generation out of date.

"Short for creepy-crawly," Simon said. "It's those eyes—the way they can make you feel, like spiders running down your spine. He makes out he's being generous—free samples, nice prices—but there's something behind it all. Not exactly a threat, not like *you'd better deal or else*...more like *I know you better than you know yourself*. What would you call him?"

Brewer thought about the impossibly dark, impossibly empty but unsettling eyes. "I don't know," he confessed. He thought about Jenny's miraculously blue eyes and marvelously clear skin, and added: "Whatever he's come up with, it cuts deeper than happy pills or dream machines."

"I could try to get some for you," Simon said. He was obviously anxious to make up for petty treasons past now that he knew what Brewer was capable of, violence-wise.

"You're too late," Brewer told him, grimly. "I already got my free sample." He went to the drawer where Simon

171

kept his collection and grabbed a handful of the advertising cards. He threw them at Simon, then went back for a second handful.

"I want a number, Simon," he said. "I want to meet a girl with a bruise just like mine but older—a lot older."

Simon was about to protest that he hadn't any idea which girl went with which card, but he thought better of it. He was a dedicated hobbyist, after all; he had a collector's pride. It took him a couple of minutes, but he found what he was looking for. Brewer took it.

"You'd better get that great gaping hole in your window fixed," Brewer told the boy. "There's a terrible draught in here."

* * * * * * *

When his staff turned up the following morning Brewer told them to drop everything else and concentrate on a rush job. They didn't ask any questions; they would assume that it was an industrial espionage job beyond the pale of legality, but it wasn't the first time they'd done that kind of work and it wouldn't be the last. They went to it with a will; it was a welcome break from the usual routine.

It only took Brewer fifteen minutes to recover the data Jenny's boyfriend had erased. As soon as he had it he passed it on to Johanna. "If you can figure out what they're for," he said. "You win a nice prize. You won't find anything like them in the patent files, but there has to be something, somewhere that will give us a clue. A protein is a protein is a protein."

"Any clues?" Johanna asked.

"They might be something to do with tissue-rejuvenation, but not in any of the conventional approaches."

She raised her eyebrows at that and glanced at the little bladder-packs on his desk, which were full of rich red blood. He nodded. "Same sort of thing," he said. "Field tests are already under way. That's why we have a lot of catching up to do. The compounds you're looking at are probably supportive; I'm going after the chap they support."

172

That was another clue and she acknowledged it with a nod. She knew that a "chap", in this context, was probably a virus vector—something that had to be kept in a suspension containing living tissue.

If Johanna saw the mark on Brewer's neck she didn't give it a second glance; she probably thought he'd spent the night with a girl. He had, of course, spent the last few hours of darkness with a sleepy whore, but she hadn't been in the least amorous. She'd been very expensive, but not by virtue of her business acumen; her reluctance to talk had been perfectly genuine—but she was, after all, a whore. It had only been a matter of fixing the right price.

The whore hadn't known Marklow's name. She'd only seen him three times. He'd been very polite, she said, but there was something about those eyes—as if they could look right into you and see the blood coursing through your veins. Jenny had persuaded her to take part in the "secret experiment", using her own improved appearance as a lure. The drug had been pitched to her as a cosmetic treatment, not as any kind of elixir of life: plastic surgery without the knife.

"A couple of days after the first shot I got itchy," the whore had told him. "Jenny told me to expect that, and not to scratch, but I couldn't help scratching a bit. It keeps coming back, especially on sunny days, and I have to wear sunglasses all day except when it's cloudy, but I've got more used to it and the pills help. I feel a bit nauseous too, mostly in the mornings—like I was pregnant. Lost weight nice and steady, but that's partly the high-protein diet. I don't mind the itching, really—it's like I can feel it working. It *is* working."

"Nothing else?" Brewer had asked, insistently.

"Only the dreams," she told him. "Jenny warned me about those, too, but I like them. They're fun."

"What kind of dreams?"

"Vampire dreams. Nightmares, some might say, but they don't scare me."

"Vampire dreams? What's that supposed to mean?" Somehow, he'd wished he could be more surprised by the introduction of *that* word.

"Sometimes, I dream I'm a bat—well, not a bat, exactly, but something like a bat. Flying by night, seeing but not seeing. Other times, I'm more like a wolf. You should see the moon! Huge and red as blood. It's great. The hunt, the kill, lapping up the blood. If that's how animals feel, I want to come back as a lion. Jenny says it's just the diet, but I reckon it's memories of other lives coming to the surface. Why else would we all have the same dreams? These shrinks who take you back to Roman times and ancient Egypt are full of crap. We were animals for billions of years, you know, before we ever became human. Race memory, isn't that what they call it?"

Brewer hadn't bothered to inform her that neither bats nor wolves were numbered among the human race's remoter ancestors. He had agreed with her that shrinks practicing past-life regression were full of crap, but hadn't added that, in his opinion, her own theory was by no means empty of it. He'd been too busy thinking about the dreams. They were the oddest thing of all—and thus, perhaps, the most significant. He remembered the haunted look in Jenny's blue eyes. One reason why she'd taken him home was to make him see how well she'd done since he dumped her, but there had been another. Whatever had been done to her had made her anxious, and a little bit lonely.

Was that, he wondered, the effect of her vampire dreams?

Brewer hadn't felt any itching yet, but he wasn't in any hurry and he didn't intend to go out in daylight until he had the problem cracked, at least insofar as it could be cracked by the equipment in the lab. Nor was he intending to sleep, let alone to dream. He was a chemist, after all; he had ways of avoiding the need for sleep at least for a couple of days.

He knew that he couldn't go back to Andrew Marklow without a deal to make, and he wasn't sure yet what kind of deal there was to be made. A promise of silence wasn't enough, for him or for Marklow. Marklow wasn't afraid that he'd go to the authorities—and not just because he figured Brewer couldn't do that without imperiling his own illicit operation. Marklow wasn't afraid, period. Brewer admired that, but it also made him anxious. Despite his chemical ex-

pertise, he'd never come close to mastering the art of not being afraid.

As things turned out, it didn't take a genius to locate the
stranger in the blood-samples. The "chap" wasn't a virus at
all; he was something much bigger. If he'd had a cell-wall
he'd have qualified as a bog-standard bacterium but he
didn't. The only label Brewer knew that might apply to him
was *rickettsia*.

The only rickettsia Brewer knew, even by repute, was
the one that caused Rocky Mountain spotted fever, but when
he went to the on-line encyclopedia he found that there were
a dozen more on record—none of which bore any very intimate resemblance to the one that had now taken up residence
somewhere in the vicinity of his brain, and was presumably
reproducing like crazy as well as retuning his endocrinal or-
chestra.

There were, Brewer noted, two significant properties
that rickettsias had. Having no cell-walls, they were immune
to antibiotics. By the same token, however, they were very
difficult to transfer from host to host. That was why Rocky
Mountain spotted fever, although incurable, hadn't ever
managed to cause an epidemic. People who caught it had it
for life—which hadn't been very long in the days before
doctors developed palliatives for the nastier symptoms—but
they didn't usually pass it on to others. Even their spouses
weren't significantly endangered; it wasn't an STD. Theory
said you could only get infected through a open cut—or, of
course, a hypodermic syringe, dumb or smart.

Brewer hesitated for a few minutes before giving the information he had gleaned to Johanna and Leroy, but he figured that the time for keeping things strictly to himself was
past. Until he had been infected there'd been no urgency at
all. Now that he'd found out that what he had was exactly
the same as what the whore had—and presumably, therefore,
exactly what Jenny had—the urgency was somewhat less
than it might have been, but time was still pressing. He
needed all the reliable help he could get.

"If you want a DNA-profile of something that big,"
Johanna pointed out, "It'll take us weeks. Maybe months.
Even if it's a variant of one of the recorded species we'd

have to start from scratch. Nobody's ever sequenced a rickettsia—or if they have, they haven't published. Do you think the pill-proteins are products of the rickettsial genes?"

"No," said Brewer. "I suspect that the pill-proteins are meant to alleviate some of the symptoms of the rickettsial infection." If that was true, it wasn't good news. It meant that he needed the pills himself if he were to enjoy the benign effects of his minuscule passengers without suffering the downside of their presence in his system.

"Infection?" Johanna echoed, anxiously. It was one of the words that always sounded alarm bells in a lab like this, even when nothing was cooking but everyday commercial products sent for routine checking.

"It's okay," he assured her. "You can only catch it through an open cut, and it's difficult even then. This one's supposed to be benign, but there has to be a catch."

"There's a catch all right," she said—but she was only talking about the '98 protocols regarding the legality of engineering human-infective agents. Nobody expected them to hold, even in the medium term. Everybody in the business knew someone, somewhere, who was working in the confident expectation that the new millennium would bring in a whole new set of rules and regulations, elastic enough to license anything, provided that it were done discreetly. Andrew Marklow might be ahead of his time, but not that far ahead of it.

The only problem, Brewer thought, was that breaking into other people's labs and shooting human-infective agents into their carotid arteries couldn't meet anyone's definition of "discretion".

"I don't need a gene-map," he told Johanna. "I just need everything we can get before nightfall."

"What happens at nightfall?" she asked.

"I have to see a man about a disease," he replied, as the phone at his elbow began to ring. He picked it up immediately, but it was only a message telling him where to go to collect a message from Talinn.

* * * * * * *

It was Jenny who answered when Brewer presented himself at the door of Marklow's building, and Jenny who came to the apartment door when he'd negotiated his way through the various layers of security. The first thing she said to him was: "You're a thief."

"And you're a whore," he said, "but we've both been taken for a ride. Your boyfriend always knew I'd come looking for him. He didn't move in on my operation to make a little extra money; he did it to attract my attention."

"Don't flatter yourself, Bru," she replied—but he wasn't flattering himself. He knew that he'd already been penciled in for recruitment when Jenny's urge to show off and rub his nose in what he'd lost had kicked things off prematurely. Sooner or later, he'd have been invited up here, and presented with an offer he couldn't refuse.

The man who called himself Anthony Marklow was standing by the window looking out over the river. He didn't offer to shake hands and he didn't offer Brewer a drink. Nor did Jenny; she just went to the settee and threw herself down in an exaggeratedly careless manner she'd probably borrowed from some American super-soap. Brewer remained standing, so that he could meet Count Dracula face to face.

Brewer was reasonably certain by now that Marklow *was* Count Dracula—maybe not literally, but as near as made no difference. His friendly neighborhood hackers hadn't managed to prove the case—in fact, they'd been so embarrassed about their failure to come up with anything concrete regarding Marklow's true identity that they'd forsaken half their fee, which had only left them enough stuff to stay high till 2020—but the void of information they'd exposed was far too deep to be any mere accident. The fact that computers had only been around for a couple of generations meant that, in theory, the early history of anyone over fifty could be utterly untraceable, but the absence of anyone behind the Marklow mask was far more pronounced than that.

"You said that you weren't convinced when Jenny told you I was serious about the genetic revolution," Brewer said, when the other transfixed him with those dark persuasive eyes, "but you did want to be convinced, didn't you?"

"I was interested," Marklow admitted. "It's time for me to move my personal project on to a bigger stage, and it would be very convenient to have some expert help."

"You took a big risk," Brewer said. "Suppose I were to start looking for a cure? I could find one, you know, given time. Just because rickettsia are immune to conventional antibiotics doesn't mean that they can't be stopped. Big bugs have little bugs upon their backs to bite 'em...."

"And little bugs have littler bugs, and so *ad infinitum*," Marklow finished for him. "It *is* a problem. You're just a small-time hack with delusion of grandeur, but there are plenty of researchers out there with the equipment and the knowledge necessary to tailor a virus to attack the agent. I've been safe from harassment for a long time, but the race will soon be on again."

"Again?" Brewer queried. He was pretty sure that he knew what Marklow meant, but he wanted confirmation.

What the vampire meant was there had been a time when he had been utterly ignorant of the nature of his own condition, quite incapable of controlling it. In those days, he must have been very vulnerable, even though the legions of would-be van Helsings who'd have staked him, beheaded him or burned him undead had even less understanding than he had. Brewer still wanted to hear him confirm all that, and he also wanted to know what sort of timescale they were talking about. He wanted to know how long Count Dracula, *alias* Andrew Marklow, had been undead, because he wanted to know what kind of life-expectancy he and Jenny might now have—or might yet obtain, as the prototype was refined and perfected.

For the time being, though, Marklow had no intention of giving too much away. First, he wanted to hear what Brewer had to say—and if the expression in his eyes was anything to go by, what Brewer said was going to have to be good. The age of Jurassic crack-dealers might be long gone, but there were still plenty of individuals in the world who could and would kill without compunction, and without the least fear of reprisal.

"I took a little nap before I came out," Brewer said, hoping that he sounded sufficiently relaxed. "I wanted to see what the dreams were like. I wasn't convinced that anything could actually do that: play dreams inside a man's head like tapes playing on a VCR. But that's what animal dreams are like, isn't it? In animals the arena of dreams is straightforwardly functional; it's for practicing instinctive behaviors and connecting up the appropriate neurochemical payoffs. It's for putting the pleasure into the necessities of life. For a few minutes, I even wondered whether the whore might be right and it might actually be an ancestral memory of some kind, secreted into a vector by accident...but that still didn't make sense. Bats and wolves aren't related that way."

Marklow nodded, but there was no sign of approval in his brooding stare.

"After that," Brewer said, "I wondered about the possibility of an extraterrestrial origin—alien DNA strayed from a meteorite or a crashed UFO—but that was only because I'd watched too much television. The real answer was much simpler. I only had to remember the *other* disease that operates the same way—and works the trick even though it's a mere virus, fifty genes short of a chromosome."

He paused for dramatic effect. It was Jenny who obligingly said: "What other disease?"

"Rabies," Brewer told her. "You see, the rabies virus isn't very infectious. Even if it's dumped straight into an open wound, with a supportive supply of saliva, it frequently fails to take, and in order to achieve that, it has to bring about some pretty extreme behavior-modifications in its victims. Hydrophobia, reckless aggression...a whole new set of meta-instincts. That's the price of its survival. It's a hell of a clumsy way to get by. Who'd have thought that a mechanism like that could have evolved *twice*? Perhaps it didn't. Perhaps the virus is just a spin-off from the rickettsia. Perhaps what you and I have is the Daddy rabies, and the one the mad dogs have is just the prodigal son."

"I don't have any kind of rabies," she told him, frostily. She wasn't nearly as outraged as Brewer had hoped she'd be.

"No," Brewer said, "You don't—not as long as you keep taking the palliatives. Even then...this is a carefully-engineered strain, selected to keep the good effects while losing the bad ones. But Mr. Marklow has a kind of rabies—

don't you, Mr. Marklow? You have the original—the kind of rabies that our ancestors called vampirism."

"I *had* the disease *your* ancestors called vampirism," Marklow riposted. "Now, I only have a modified form of it, which is much more like the strain with which the subjects of my field-trial have been infected. You might say that I'd been cured, provided that you weren't too fussy about the definition of the word *cure*. I've traded an awkward but valuable infection for its civilized cousin, which is equally valuable but far less awkward."

"How much less awkward?" Brewer wanted to know.

"Did you bring the results of your analyses?" the ex-vampire countered.

Brewer pulled a sheaf of papers out of the inside pocket of his jacket. It was only a dozen sheets of A4 but there was a lot of data packed into the dozen sheets and he'd summarized his conclusions very tersely.

While Marklow looked at the data, Brewer studied Jenny, searching for the slightest indication of an unfortunate side-effect. The mark on her neck told him that she still needed booster-shots—that even if it were shot right into the carotid artery the rickettsia still had difficulty taking up permanent residence in the brain and its associated structures—but that wasn't bad news. If he were to carry forward Marklow's grand scheme for the remaking of human nature, he could certainly maintain his supplies of the rickettsia, given that he had a readily-available culture-medium.

"That's good," Marklow said, when he'd scanned the familiar information and read the judgmental comments. "Your staff evidently make up an effective team, and you obviously trust them. How much of the whole picture have you let them see?"

"They know that there's a whole new approach to rejuvenative technology and life-extension—and they have enough of a basis to start their own research along the same lines, individually or in alliance. They don't know that the new approach is really an old approach. They know I got the data from somewhere else but they think it was one more commission. They don't know that it was a gift from Count Dracula. They don't know that one of the blood-bags was mine, so they don't know I'm a carrier. *How much less awkward?*"

Marklow smiled. It wasn't a particularly predatory smile. "I no longer have any real compulsion to bite or stab my fellow creatures and apply my slavering lips to the wounds," he said. "The dreams still frighten me a little—I don't suppose I'll ever be able to take the innocent pleasure in them that my new generation of converts can—but they're no longer a curse that I have to fight with every last vestige of my strength."

He paused briefly. The expression in his eyes was unfathomable but his voice was gentle and regretful. "I did have to fight it, you know," he said, sounding as if he genuinely wanted to be believed. "It was the price of survival in the modern world. I had to remain hidden, unknown...I had to become a figure of legend, a mere superstition. I saw what happened to others of my kind who couldn't master their appetites. There are a thousand ways to die, you see, even for... someone like me. We did our best to spread rumors to the contrary, but *our* rumors always had to compete with *theirs*. The confusion worked to our benefit, in some ways, but not in others...."

"I've been alone for a long time, but I knew that science would save me. I knew that there would be a revolution some day that would allow me to transcend my monstrousness and become a true immortal. I knew that, when that happened, I could rejoin the human race and become its benefactor, changing evil into good. I knew that there would come a time when I could look for company again—for congenial company."

Brewer wasn't sure whether the adjective referred to Jenny, or to him, or to both of them, but he couldn't resist the temptation to feign misunderstanding. "I guess a cohort of whores is about as congenial as you can get," he said, "if you're that way inclined."

He cast a calculatedly negligent glance in Jenny's direction, and saw that he had wounded her, but Marklow remained unmoved. If the ex-vampire was as old as Brewer suspected, he was probably unmovable. He'd probably been undead for a very long time—but at least he'd had nightmares all the while. There had been a taint of Hell in his un-holy existence, and might be still, even in a world that was on the verge of conquering all the Hells of old: disease, death, pain and misery.

"Where should I have looked for volunteers?" Marklow asked, in all apparent earnest. "Prisons? Cardboard City?"

"Old people's homes?" Brewer countered, not at all ear-nestly. "Not sufficiently unobtrusive, I suppose. You do plan to remain unobtrusive, I suppose, even when you start seri-ous marketing. The rich will want to keep it to themselves, of course. They appreciate confidentiality. Vampires, the lot of them—they think of mere human beings as cattle. That's why you thought of me when you wondered how best to ex-pand your operation, I suppose. You think I'm a kind of vampire too, because I sell illegal happy pills to pimps and whores, kids and hackers."

"You're not any real kind of vampire yet," Marklow re-sponded, mildly. "You'll have to work at it. It sometimes takes half a dozen shots before the rickettsias are perma-nently established. But once they're set, they're set for life—and that could be a long time."

"How long?" Brewer wanted to know.

"We'll just have to wait and see," Count Dracula told him. "We're dealing with a new strain, after all."

"How good was the old strain?" Brewer persisted.

"I don't know," Marklow replied. "The oldest men I ever knew had forgotten long ago how old they were. Arith-metic hadn't been invented when they were young. Nor had writing—but fire had. Fire and wooden spears. By the time writing was invented the war was almost lost. The rickettsia almost went the way of the mammoth and the saber-toothed tiger, and the thousand other species neolithic man hounded to extinction. Mercifully, it survived. Mercifully, I survived with it. Now, the new era is dawning. Soon, I won't have to hide any more. Together, you and I and all of Jenny's friends...we shall be the midwives of the *übermensch*, as you so tactfully put it."

Brewer could see that Jenny felt uncomfortable. She knew that an important boundary had been crossed when Marklow first allowed the word "vampire" to cross his lips.

182

He was exposed now, and so was she. She was afraid—but Marklow wasn't. He had grown out of fear long ago. He still retained the ability to terrify, but he couldn't identify with those he terrified. He gave the impression of knowing more about his victims than they knew themselves, but he didn't. He thought that he was still, essentially, a man—but he didn't know *human* beings at all. Perhaps it had been a mistake for him to try so hard to become harmless, to become a saint instead of a devil.

"Togetherness," Brewer told him, sardonically, "is a wonderful thing."

Bang on cue, the doorbell rang. Not the bell that rang when someone was downstairs, outside the reinforced doors of the building, but the discreet chime which signaled that someone was at the door of the apartment.

Marklow knew as well as Brewer did that anyone with the skill to get that far without being detected didn't need to sound the chime—that the gesture was a kind of mockery.

"Don't get up," Brewer said to Jenny. "I think that's for me."

* * * * * * *

Brewer had instructed the man with the rifle not to take any chances; he had seen how quickly Marklow could move and how powerfully he could hit out. The marksman fired as soon as he was sure of his shot, and Marklow slumped to the floor.

It was the shock of the impact that had felled him, but the ex-vampire's attempt to rise to his feet was all in vain. The tranquillizer-dart would have sent a horse to sleep, or even a tiger.

"Look after him," Brewer said, as the collection-squad went to pick up the body. "He's an endangered species. Make sure you put him in a nice strong cage—and be careful when he wakes up. I dare say he can still bite, when the mood takes him."

Jenny had got up from the settee. She still looked like a minor character in some Hollywood super-soap, but now she seemed to think that her face was in close-up and that her features had better start running the gamut of the emotions, at least from Alarm to Anxiety.

Brewer held the door open for the man from the ministry. "Jenny, this is Mr. Smith," he said, over his shoulder. "He wants to you to give him a complete list of all the friends you introduced to Mr. Marklow. It probably won't matter much if it isn't quite complete, but you'd gain a good deal of moral credit if it were—and from here on in, it might be a good idea not to be overdrawn at the moral credit bank. I told your boyfriend the truth when I said that I could design a cure for what you have, given time and a big enough budget. If you want to hang on to your indigenous rickettsias you'll have to make yourself useful."

Mr. Smith didn't smile. Brewer hadn't expected him to. Men from the ministry—*any* ministry—lost their smiling reflexes once they'd been in the job for a while.

"You bastard," Jenny said. "You sold us out!"

Brewer put on a show of being deeply wounded. "*I* sold *you* out! You were the one who told your new boyfriend all about my covert operations. You sold him my...business associates. You even sold him your old friends, as bankrupt stock at a knockdown price. Then he wanders into my top-security lab, calm as you please, beats me up and shoots me full of bugs—bugs whose not-so-remote ancestors have had him chewing bloody holes in anything and everything warm-blooded for hundreds, if not thousands, of years. Did he really think that was the right way to win me over—or was it your idea? You never did understand human nature, and he must have forgotten everything he learned when he was human himself. Not entirely surprising, I suppose, given that his disease made him closer kin to mad dogs and vampire bats. The only element of social intercourse he mastered was the art of staying hidden, masked by a legend that had become a joke...and in the end he even forgot that."

Jenny looked back at him with eyes that were almost as piercing, almost as threatening, as Anthony Marklow's—but they were still baby blue in color, and she hadn't quite enough presence to carry off the act. She wasn't a real vampire, after all. She only had bad dreams.

"I thought you meant it," she said, feebly. "I really thought you meant all that stuff about being at the cutting edge of the next revolution—about the quest for immortality, the transcendence of all inherited limitations."

"I did mean it," he told her. "I still do. What do you think I'm doing here? It's a question of quality control. Did you think I could entrust this kind of work, and the rewards that are likely to flow from it, to someone like *him*? He's a fucking *vampire*, for God's sake!"

Jenny's burning gaze flickered from Brewer to the un-smiling Mr. Smith and back again, as if to say: *What's he? What kind of quality control does he represent?*

What she actually said was: "Anthony would have cut you in. He'd have made you an equal partner. The establishment won't even cut you in. As soon as I tell this creep what he wants to know, you and I will be surplus to requirements. They'll have it all."

"You watch too much television," Brewer told her. "The government isn't a conspiracy set up to control us. I *voted* for the government. I sure as hell never voted for Count Dracula. And your slang's out of date. Nobody except Simple Simon calls people *creeps* any more—and Simon's so sad he gets off on collecting the business cards from public phone booths."

"You couldn't stand it, could you?" she retorted. "You just couldn't stand seeing me like this. People you throw away are supposed to stay thrown away, aren't they Bru? They aren't supposed to find someone better, to get their lives back on track. You did this because you're jealous— bitter and twisted and jealous."

Brewer had to check Mr. Smith's face to make sure that he hadn't cracked a smirk. Mr. Smith was being very patient, even by the standards customarily observed by the establishment's bureaucrats.

"We have to leave, Jenny," Brewer said, quietly. "There are people waiting outside. They have to search the place, collect all *this*." He waved a negligent hand at the books and CDs.

"They have no right," she whispered—but she didn't press the point. How could she? She knew as well as Brewer

185

did that Anthony Marklow was guilty of any number of crimes, recent as well as ancient. She wasn't innocent herself—not according to the '98 protocols. In fact, she was a dangerous felon, not to mention a willing carrier of an illegally-engineered organism.

Brewer waited for her to fall into step with the man from the ministry and then he followed them, at a respectful distance.

He was confident that Jenny was wrong about him being a fool to trust the legitimate authorities. After all, he really had voted for them—and he'd taken care to post twenty copies of his twelve A-4 sheets to secret repositories all over the world, routed via Talinn and Tokyo, Ratzeburg and Palermo. Given that the net was still in its frontier phase, the chances of his new colleagues being able to locate and destroy them all were pretty slim.

He wished that he'd made more progress in the art of being intimidating, but he knew that even if he'd been a real gangster he couldn't possibly have come to a different decision. Even gangsters couldn't be entirely immune to the duties of citizenship; they were as dependent as anyone else on the solidarity and stability of the social order. The way he'd chosen would lead to wealth, and hence to power, as surely as any other—and by way of a bonus he'd have a special kind of fame thrown in.

From now until the end of time he'd be known as the man who'd finally put an end to the evil career of Count Dracula: the man who'd exposed the last undead vampire in the West for what he truly was.

A reputation like that would surely be enough to make eternal life worth living.

WORSE THAN THE DISEASE

The trouble with living and loving in the Age of Recreational Disease is that you have to be very careful what company you keep. Some people have very strange ways of enjoying themselves, and there are some truly sick individuals around, whose idea of enjoying themselves is to stop others from doing likewise.

I like to think that I'm as liberal as the next man. I don't mind the usual kinds of diseases—the ones that come with the Official Government Health Warning. Anything you can buy across the counter in Boots and take by mouth, with a sweet to take the taste away, is perfectly okay by me. I've tried a few of the popular ones and I have to say that I think they're over-rated by the fashion gurus, but as long as they stay where they're put and aren't contagious I don't have any objection at all to people using them—even kids. We're living in the twenty-first century and we have to take an enlightened view of such things.

Where I draw the line, though—and where the line really has to be drawn for everybody, in my opinion—is the kind of disease that you can pass on to other people. What people do to themselves is entirely up to them, but when they start inflicting it on others they're definitely out of order. I'm not talking about the far-out crazies of the DLF—just ordinary people who are plain downright irresponsible.

The things that can be spread by coughs and sneezes are bad enough, but the worst betrayal of trust by far is when a person deliberately passes on an STD. I know that some people get an extra kick out of sex if they do it while they're infectious, but that seems to me to be the kind of kick that's simply perverse. Some people say that it doesn't really mat-

187

ter, given that everything is curable nowadays, but it's not as simple as that. It's a mistake to think that all cures return you to the condition you were in before. Sometimes they don't.

Sometimes they can't.

I met this woman a little while ago. Her name was Sarah. She was slim and sweet and eminently desirable—and she was carrying a really heavy-duty mutant STD. When I say "carrying", I mean *carrying*. She was an authentic Typhoid Mary, suffering only the slightest of symptoms and offering no immunological response to the virus. It was the kind of thing that's only supposed to last a fortnight, even if it's left untreated, but Sarah had played host to it for years. That's one of the problems with recreational diseases, you see—just like real diseases, they don't take everybody the same way. What some people can live with in peaceful equilibrium reduces others to physical and mental wreckage.

I'd like to think that Sarah simply didn't understand that what was harmless to her wasn't harmless to others, but it wouldn't be true. I'm pretty sure that she knew exactly what she was doing, and got a thrill out of it. Maybe she thought it was funny that something that didn't hurt her at all could have such a profound effect on others.

I thought she really liked me! Even at the end, when I found out I'd been infected, she acted as if she'd done me a favor, for affection's sake.

"People like you don't realize how narrow and tawdry their lives are," she said. "I'm just broadening your existential horizons a little. If you don't like it, all you have to do is take the shots."

To Sarah, it was as simple as that—but not to me.

What the virus did was to screw up the pituitary and the hypothalamus in such a way as to alter the neurochemical balance of my emotions. Maybe I reacted more extremely than others whose existential horizons she'd broadened, but I doubt it. I took the shots as soon as I figured out what was happening, but I still had to suffer the symptoms until the antiviruses could bring my system back to normal.

Pleasure went right out the window, reduced from a perfectly healthy day-by-day thrill to absolute zero. On its own, that wouldn't have been particularly problematic—I could have used common-or-garden uppers to treat the symptom while the antiviruses got to work on the cause—but that was only part of it. The decrease in pleasure was countered by a dramatic increase in grief and envy. That wasn't so easy to treat with palliatives, partly because it wasn't just a matter of degree.

I started feeling sorrowful about the weirdest things. I felt sad about the gradual diminishing of the soap on the side of the wash-basin. The brokenness of the white line down the middle of the road brought me to the brink of tears. I actually broke down sobbing when the sun was eclipsed by a fluffy white cloud. I had to leave the TV on all day and all night because I couldn't bear to switch it off. Cooking became an absolute nightmare, in spite of the fact that I took care to avoid anything remotely fresh.

The world seemed so full of tragedy that I thought my heart would break.

The envy was even worse. I began to envy oak trees their mistletoe, and cats the loving bite of their fleas. The sight of a photocopier sucking sheets of paper out of the feeder would drive me to paroxysms of jealousy. Every time I heard a phone ring I was transfixed by the angry knowledge that I couldn't sing as sweetly. Everything I needed, and didn't have, seemed to be in the possession of unworthy animals, stupid plants and inanimate objects, all of which were utterly and insultingly oblivious of their awesome good fortune.

It seemed as if I were spending half my waking moments in tears and the rest grinding my teeth in jealous rage. The only breaks I had from abject misery were intervals of fervent envy, and the only breaks I had from wrathful contemplation of the precious possessions of absurd objects were the hours when I couldn't stem the flood of my deepest sympathies for the piteous plights of the very same entities.

There aren't any efficient palliatives available for those sorts of symptoms. Downers only intensified my sorrow, and uppers only sharpened my envy. Unless I was prepared to spend an entire week under general anesthesia I simply had to hang on while the antiviruses got to grips with the bogey in every infected cell.

189

Had I know then what I know now I'd have opted for the general anesthesia but I was stubbornly determined not to fold up under the pressure.

"How bad can it get?" I said to the doctor, in a blithely rhetorical fashion. "It's not as if it were chronic asthma or gas gangrene, is it?"

Unfortunately, the virus was just as stubborn as I was. I had three relapses before my immune system, aided and abetted by the best antiviruses money could buy, finally came through for me. At first, the doctor assured me that the antiviruses would clear up the trouble inside forty-eight hours, but two days became four, then eight. By the time I was finally free of it I was beginning to think that I might as well have let it run its course.

I lost eighteen pounds and all my dignity.

The last time I spoke to Sarah she told me that she hadn't meant to hurt me at all, and that all the stuff about broadening my existential horizons had been bullshit. All she'd really wanted, she said, was to make sure I wouldn't ever forget her. She succeeded. I might have made a real mess of her face if I hadn't had a sneaking suspicion that she'd rejigged her nervous system so that she could enjoy that kind of thing.

I'm over the STD now, of course. Physically, I'm back to normal. There are no organic after-effects at all. Any residual problems I have a purely psychological—but the trouble is, you see, that you can't *forget* something like that, and you can't entirely unlearn the experience.

Once you've been reduced to the depths of anguish by the slow melting of a bar of soap, and once you've been plunged into a hell of jealousy by the fact that a cat has fleas, it's not easy to re-orchestrate your responses in the ordinary way.

My mother died last week, and I can't seem to feel a damn thing—it means no more to me than the fact that the white line down the middle of the road has gaps in it, or the fact that clouds occasionally pass across the face of the sun.

You might think that that would be the worst of it, but you'd be wrong. I didn't suppose I'd ever miss the ability to be envious, but when nothing that anyone else has—money, possessions, status, beauty, intelligence—seems any more important than the paper consumed by a photocopier, or the plaintive song of a telephone, it becomes well nigh impossible to want anything at all.

I can feel pleasure again now, but I can't desire what I don't have and I can't grieve for anything I lose. Maybe it'll all come back, in time, but it'll take a lot longer than a fortnight.

If you want to know what Hell is like, I can tell you. It's what I've had to come back to now that I've been cured.

If you ever run into Sarah, don't bother to give her my love—and be very careful how you dispose of your own. We may have domesticated disease, but we aren't yet the masters of ease.

www.ingramcontent.com/pod-product-compliance
Lightning Source LLC
Chambersburg PA
CBHW032010240626
47153CB00003B/1199